The back of his left hand itched a few minutes later. He scratched at it idly, remembering the splinters he'd sucked out of it and the stinging sap, like mild acid on his skin. The booze must have dampened the itch earlier but now he noticed it, it was the only thing he could think about.

His scratching didn't help; if anything, it made matters worse and now he was convinced he had something worming around in there, immediately under his skin, something he had to get out.He rubbed harder then scratched his fingernails, hard, over his knuckles but he only exacerbated the itch.

He used all the nails of his right hand, scratching up and down from fingertips up to almost the wrist but the itch spread apace with his scrubbing.When he looked down his left hand was red, blotchy, much worse than it had been under the influence of the sap and looking like it had taken some serious sunburn. Worse though, the large arteries under the skin were darker still, not red but brown, almost black and thick, as if someone had been tracing there with a Sharpie.

When he tried to flex his fingers he met stiffening resistance, as if the blood had gone solid.There was no pain but the stiffening was worsening and within seconds his left hand went rigid. He tried to make a fist but he couldn't move his fingers. His hand was unresponsive to any commands, curled over, almost claw like.

THE GREEN
AND
THE BLACK

BY WILLIAM MEIKLE

1

They'd bounced along the rutted track for more than an hour. The back axle creaked, complained and held.

Keith had never been more thankful for the University's efficiency in maintaining its trucks. They had been lucky at the pound; this pickup was newer than most, a big GM beast. It roared like a bull-moose, guzzled gas like a thirsty elephant yet cruised at a hundred and twenty like a cheetah in its prime.

Five hours into the trip and he hadn't felt tired or stressed. It was like traveling in a comfortable armchair and was by far the most pleasant driving experience Keith had ever had, or at least it had been right up until they'd driven onto the rutted track.

They hadn't met any other traffic since turning off the blacktop at Buchans, which was probably for the good as there was nowhere on this stretch where they could easily turn around. The track was only as wide as their truck, a deep ditch ran along the passenger side and thick birch scrub filled the view outside Keith's own driver's side window. Keith took it as slow as he could although some of the ruts and holes were likely to see them brought to a standstill if he tried to take them too carefully.

The Professor looked completely unconcerned about the terrain. The older man in the passenger seat kept up a stream of talk for the benefit of the three students in the back, giving them details about their destination and its history and what they hoped to find. Keith had to keep his eyes ahead; the track was narrowing even more. Damp branches clutched at his wing mirror and slapped on the roof as they went under the canopy.

"How much farther, Professor?" he asked. "It's too tight

here. If it gets any narrower some those branches are going to tangle up in the wheel arches. I know this truck's a beast but there are limits."

"Not long now." The professor had a map out on his knees and measured the distance between thumb and forefinger. "Two, maybe three kilometers, no more than that."

"I'm not sure we'll get there," Keith said but the Professor had already returned to talking to the students in the back.

"This is your heritage, lads. You're all from local Irish families, aren't you? I know Keith is German from way back and I'm from Scottish stock myself. So, this trip is for you."

It was the smallest and normally quietest of the three, Gerry who spoke up first. Keith had been surprised when Gerry volunteered for the long weekend trip; he was normally the reserved one in their class of twelve and last to put himself forward. Yet here he was piping up again. Some students worked better in smaller, more intimate groups. Gerry was possibly one of them. If so this trip was going to prove it, one way or the other.

"Yeah, my family came over in the famine years, about eighteen fifty," Gerry said. "Dan here tells me I'm an interloper as his family has been here since God knows how long before that."

Dan spoke up next. In contrast to Gerry, Dan was the brash one. He was popular and he knew it, self-confident, maybe a touch too much so for Keith's liking, for it sometimes came with a bragging swagger that looked too much like bullying.

"My great to the sixth or seventh great granddad came over as a whaler and stayed, sometime in the late seventeen hundreds, according to my ma." He playfully punched Bill on the shoulder. "Beats this one's family by twenty years at a guess. Yeah, we're all Irish in the back here, to be sure, boyo."

Bill said nothing. Keith wasn't surprised. He was usually the foil for Dan's jokes, loyal sidekick in the main but only speaking up when Dan wasn't around to dominate the conversation.

"The men who worked the mine we're looking for were all Irish too," the professor began again and went into the louder yet softer toned voice he used while lecturing. "Or so we've been led to believe by the report Keith and I found."

Keith had heard this bit several times before. It was why he'd agreed to the trip. They'd uncovered the possibility of an old mining camp of Irish prospectors from the eighteen seventies, a mystery to solve and the chance to get out of town for a bit and away from his troubles. It was almost too good to be true.

The Professor hadn't said anything about driving through terrain like this though. The track was only marginally wide enough to accommodate the truck now and more branches tugged and whipped at it. The paint job was going to be scratched and scuffed all along the driver's side. Although they hadn't had to put down any kind of deposit on the vehicle, there had been dire warnings of consequences if it didn't come back in the same state in which they took it out.

But that's the Professor's call, not mine.

Keith concentrated on the narrow space ahead, feeling like too big a bit of thread trying to get through the hole of a needle that was getting increasingly smaller. Now the foliage crept closer on both sides of them as the ditch had gone, to be replaced with more of the tight canopy.

Branches tugged at the wheel rims. He was ready to call it as a dead end and didn't relish having to reverse all the way backward when the foliage ahead abruptly thinned out and the view opened up again. The track widened as it came out of the tunnel and approached a large dark pond to Keith's right.

The Professor clapped Keith on the shoulder.

"See, I told you we were close. This must be the place."

They looked over a flat stretch of land rising up to a high rocky outcrop some two hundred meters away on the far side of the pond from them. The track ahead, little more than a slightly flatter bit of land now, ran around the edge of the water toward the outcrop.

"Where's the camp?" one of the lads in the back said. Keith had been wondering the same thing.

There was no sign anyone had been here but themselves for many years. The ground was covered all around in thick myrtle and juniper shrubs interspersed with straggly pines and lanky over-stretched specimens of birch and mountain ash. It was slightly flatter along the line of the track but it wasn't going to be too many years before there would be no sign a track had even existed. There were no recent tracks, large or small, no footprints or hoof marks; there weren't even any of the piles of moose shit that were usually omnipresent in the wild spots on the island.

"Are you sure we're in the right place, Professor?" Keith said. "It looks like a dead end to me."

The Professor laughed.

"If the report we found was accurate it's been well over a century since the mining operation, lads. It's here somewhere. Trust me." He turned to speak directly to Keith. "Follow the track around the pond here. Miners do the mining in rock, remember? The camp will be somewhere over by the outcrop or close to it. You mark my words."

Keith drove on, taking it even more carefully now. The ground was soggier here; it hadn't exactly been dry on the way along the track and despite it being summer there had been deep puddles in some of the ruts. Here at the edge of the pond the puddles had gotten organized and soaked all the surrounding area. It was more of a bog than a track in places. The truck wallowed, even threatened to sink at one point but Keith kept his momentum up and plowed on. He saw in the rear-view that he had left a double line of brown tracks in his wake, filling with dank water as he passed.

Black flies rose in lazy swarms around them, disturbed by the truck's intrusion into their domain; there was no other sign of life. Keith had brought along his rod, line and gear in the hope he might get some fishing done. The pond itself looked even less inviting than the ground; it was too dark, somehow so stagnant even the black flies ignored its surface. A light shimmer of oily vapor hung over the water above a surface that was only slightly rippled despite a stiff breeze coming from the north. If he didn't know better he'd have thought he was looking at a pool of old motor oil rather than water.

All in all, this wasn't quite the inviting wilderness to which he'd been hoping to escape.

Matters improved, although only a little, as the track veered to the left, leading away from the edge of the pond and toward the rocky outcrop to the west. The rock, a large, almost semi-spherical plug that looked like it had been dropped into the landscape from a great height, loomed high over them. Despite the fact it was only early afternoon the sun had already passed over the top, leaving a deep shade across the land between it and the pond.

At first it didn't seem like an inviting spot in which to stop and make camp but the ground was slightly raised above the water line here and drier because of it. Keith drove up a short incline onto a flat and almost level patch of gravel and grit before bringing the truck to a halt.

"As good a place as any?" he asked and the Professor smiled and nodded.

"This will do nicely." He turned to address the three in the back. "Get the tents up lads, Keith and I will scout out the area and fetch some firewood."

Keith switched off the engine, got out the pickup and stretched his back and legs. He took in a deep breath and let the quiet fill him up. Even the small slope up from the pond, five feet above water level at most, gave some protection from the black flies and the air was cold and bracing in his lungs. He felt the chill on his hands and at his ankles too but ignored it for now, taking in the view.

The pond, a long thin one, stretched away to the north, narrowing as it approached the horizon. It was completely encircled by vegetation, overhanging trees and thick shrubs. There was no sign of any jetties, housing or even a clear spot. Keith would have expected to see at least one beaver lodge on such a pond anywhere else on the island but there was only the thickly covered shoreline in all directions. Behind him, to the south and east of the rock face, was the flat piece of land they'd driven across and, beyond that, thick shrubs and twisted, stunted trees. If there had been a mining camp here, he couldn't see any sign of it now.

But he wasn't going to let it bother him at the moment. He

had to get the drive out of his system. Usually after a long time behind the wheel, the tension would take a while to wash away but the truck had been an easy ride for the most part and he was a country boy at heart. Being out in the wilds, even in such a lifeless spot as this, always lifted his spirits.

The three students were already busy unpacking the gear from the back of the truck. Normally Keith would have volunteered to help with the tents but the Professor was already walking away, not toward anywhere they might get firewood but straight for the overhanging rocky outcrop some twenty meters west of where they'd parked.

The Professor, Frank Duffett, was Keith's boss, friend and the top man in the field of the industrial archaeology of Newfoundland. Admittedly it was rather a small field, the Professor having been the only man in it until he persuaded the University they needed a small faculty some ten years ago.

Keith had only gotten into it in the first place after failing his first year of Engineering Studies due to a surfeit of partying and booze. Once the first semester began, the Professor's infectious enthusiasm won him over and Keith discovered a calling. In following the Professor in his studies, he got to spend a lot of time poking around in quiet corners of the province, the paperwork wasn't too onerous and the winter research, of necessity spent in the lab and library, was even interesting. When they'd found a letter stuck away in the Buchans' mining archive referring to an abandoned mine farther south that had never been documented, Keith had been only too keen to help arrange the trip. Besides the thrill of something new, he also hoped there might eventually be enough in it to allow him to write up a paper with the Professor on the subject.

It didn't surprise Keith in the least to see the Professor eager to get to work straight away; he felt the same.

"Hey, Keith. Which way up does this big tent go?" Gerry shouted from the rear of the truck.

"You're a big boy now. Figure it out."

He hurried away from the gravel parking area, leaving the grumbling students behind and followed quickly after the Professor, who was already grubbing around in the undergrowth between the truck and the rock face.

"See here," the Professor said as Keith arrived at his side. He pointed down to something at his feet but at first Keith only saw a stunted Juniper shrub before the Professor moved a branch aside with his foot. A heavily rusted piece of metal, two feet long, sat half-embedded in the ground, a fragment of an old rail or cart line.

"We're on the right track," the Professor said and laughed loudly at his own joke before going on. "Even if that's all we find, it's evidence there was something here worthy of further investigation. That's all we can ask for on this first trip up here."

It didn't take them more than five minutes to find more evidence that they'd arrived in the right place. On the way down the slope to look for firewood, they quickly came upon rotted timbers, basic foundations, and a shallow hole mostly filled with old dried up pieces of all too human feces marking what had obviously been a rudimentary outhouse.

More rusted tracks led from there back up the slope toward the rock face and in the other direction down the rest of the slope toward the thicker shrubs. There, behind a matted and twisted wall of ash and birch saplings, they caught a glimpse of what looked to be the remains of several rough sheds. Keith wanted to get in among those tumbled ruins and rummage right away but the Professor held him back.

"Much as I'd love to get my hands dirty now, we need to document everything on our way through this site. You never know what we'd miss if we barreled in willy-nilly. Come on. We said we'd collect firewood so we'd better get to it. Don't pick up any old timber if it looks like it might have been part of a building."

They reluctantly backed away from the denser shrubbery toward more open ground and hunted for dry wood for the fire. There were plenty of branches on the ground but most were too damp to be of use and they would have to cover a wide area before they gathered enough for a decent fire.

They split up to cover more ground so Keith was alone when he came across the copse of healthier growth, a rough circle of mountain ash that was lush and green and already, even this early in the year, showing a good crop of bright red berries. He didn't find any dry kindling though, and he was about to turn away when a movement in the crook of the ash's branches caught his eye. He turned toward it.

It must have been a trick of the light.

There was nothing alive there; but somebody alive had been in the area and not long ago by the look of it. A small figure made of twigs and leaves, no more than a foot tall, sat, legs dangling in the crook of the branches; the twigs and leaves it was made of were still fresh. The wood looked sappy, the leaves bright green starting to go yellow at the edges. As the ash's canopy moved in the breeze overhead so too did the dancing shadows and it looked like the twig doll was swinging its legs, waving its hands and smiling, with tiny green eyes staring straight into Keith's soul.

Keith turned away. He didn't trust the green-eyed smile. It reminded him too much of Joanna. He'd left her back in the city and she was probably still rightfully mad at him. The thought washed away all the good feelings he'd been building since he'd gotten out of the truck and reminded him again of the other reason why he'd agreed to come out here into the wilds with the Professor

I came here to avoid thinking about that.

He hefted the kindling in his arms tighter against his chest so he wouldn't drop any of it and made his way back to the truck, hoping the students had remembered to bring the beer.

2

Gerry Paterson looked up from the makeshift round of stones he'd laid to encircle the fire as Keith, carrying a huge pile of sticks, walked toward the small camp they'd set up. The pickup and their three tents made a rough square around a central patch of flat grit and gravel with Gerry's fireplace just off center.

Gerry had ended up figuring out how to put up the tents; Bill and Doug were worse than useless, arguing until Doug decided he was bored and sloped off for a beer. Gerry got on fine once he figured out how the fiberglass poles fit together and it only took ten minutes to get the big tent up. The other two were easy, especially with Bill's help.

Once the tents were up, Bill made straight to the pickup to join Doug and now they were already cracking their second bottles. They were only here for the course credits; Doug in particular had already made that abundantly clear but Gerry's interest had been piqued by the Professor's spiel on the way here. The idea that one of his distant relatives might have been on this spot looking for anything that would raise him up in the world meant beer was the furthest thing from Gerry's thoughts right then.

He kept busy preparing the hearth, a reminder of happier days as a youth, helping his dad build much the same kind of fire in much the same kind of spot on childhood fishing trips. Once Keith arrived beside him and dumped a load of wood on the gravel, he helped arrange some of the kindling and get a fire going and was so intent on the job that he jumped when Keith spoke, his voice suddenly loud in the quiet of the campsite.

"Where's the Professor?"

"I thought he was with you?"

"He was," Keith replied. "He should be back here by now."

They both looked up toward the rock face at the same moment.

"He wouldn't go down a mineshaft alone would he?" Gerry asked.

"If he found one? Of course, he would. But I'm hoping he's still gathering wood. I'll go and find him."

The research assistant moved as if he was going to walk out of the camp but right then the Professor came through between the pickup and the tent on the outcrop side. He wasn't carrying firewood. Instead he had a tin box in his hands, about the size of a shoebox but slightly taller. It was blackened on the side Gerry could see, as if the exterior had been burned at some point in the past but it was structurally sound enough for the Professor to carry it without it falling apart on him.

"I found something," the older man said. His smile was as broad as a kid's in a candy store with money in his pocket.

"So, the spiel about documenting our way in and out? What was that?" Keith said. He took the box from the Professor and carefully placed it down on the gravel at their feet.

The Professor kept smiling.

"I tripped over the damn thing. It was lying there under a fallen tree. I've made a note of where I found it," he patted at his breast pocket where a small notebook and two pens showed at the top, "so there's no worry. Besides... it's Day One... and we found something."

His excitement was catching, enough so that the two other students left their beers in the pickup bed and came over to watch as the Professor knelt down and carefully pried open the lid of the box with his penknife.

They all leaned forward to get a better look at the contents. Gerry was disappointed to see it was two-thirds empty and there was nothing in the bottom save for some slightly damp paper and what looked to be a small leather-bound notebook, similar in size to the one the Professor had in his pocket.

Doug, obviously unimpressed, went back to the pickup and the beer and Bill shuffled away seconds later but the Professor was rapt. Slowly, almost unbearably so, he pried open the notebook.

The pages looked crisp and dry and Gerry saw writing but was too far away to read any of it. The Professor read from the front page.

"The diary of Joseph Patrick Donnelly, begun this day of our Lord 23rd May, 1874."

"It seems I have been appointed foreman for this stage of our expedition."

The Professor kept reading, alternately checking both the notebook and the sheaves of papers in the box but had gone quiet, reading silently until Keith and Gerry couldn't take it any longer.

"For pity's sake, Professor What have we got?" Keith said.

When he looked up the Professor's grin was bigger than ever.

"We've only got a record of the work a group of Irish prospectors undertook here in 1874. A complete record, consisting of finances, stores, supplies, building materials, a roll listing the men's names, ages and addresses and Joseph's personal diary for the whole summer by the look of it. We've got enough here to recreate the whole enterprise. And I tripped over it by accident. We couldn't have hoped for a better start."

He looked down at the box of papers and the diary he still held.

"We need to get these papers bagged and tagged, each one individually. Photographed too, although we can do that again back in St John's. Keith, you take the pictures, I'll take the diary and Gerry can do the bagging and database inventory. Are we all agreed?"

Keith nodded and Gerry, still processing the fact he'd been included, managed a muttered affirmation.

Gerry spent the next few hours in the largest of the three tents, their office and workspace while they were here on site. Keith removed the papers one at a time from the tin box and carefully smoothed each one out between two sheets of clear glass for easier photographing. Once Keith had finished with each sheet Gerry removed it from between the glass panes, bagged it carefully in clear wrappers, tagged it with a sticker containing its catalog number and entered the number and a brief description of the contents in the laptop database.

For a while it was only Keith and Gerry at the camp table. The Professor had gone off with the journal to read it in private. They got into a rhythm so that the bagging and tagging went smoothly. Gerry had enough time to quickly look over some of the documents as he worked on them. The Professor had been right. It appeared they had a record of all the mining camp's activity over a period of several months, consisting of bills, work orders, the roll of the staff, even three birth certificates for men born in Ireland in the early 1850s. Some of the papers were slightly damp and the ink had faded and run in places but it looked like they had more than enough material to keep them busy over the winter months ahead and there was still the small diary to come. Who knew what information that might hold?

Gerry wanted to pore over everything there and then but the photography was going slightly faster than his tagging and he had to work fast to keep up with Keith. For a while he got lost in the rhythm of the work.

In late afternoon, the Professor came into the tent.

"I've got those other two making us something to eat," he said. "It'll keep them out of mischief and away from the beer."

He handed Keith the diary.

"You had best photograph each page separately," he said. "Although I'm not sure how much worth there is in it."

Keith raised an eyebrow.

"I thought this would be the pot of gold," he said.

"As did I," the Professor replied. "But I've had a quick skim and while there's some good stuff at the start, it turns strange after a while. I don't think the man was in his right mind. It merits a closer look but I doubt there's much of anything of use to us there. I'll read it more slowly once you've got it cataloged. Maybe it'll make more sense on a second run through it."

Keith finished up photographing the single sheets from the tin box and moved on to the diary. That involved him taking two photographs, one for each facing page and it gave Gerry a chance to catch up on the loose sheets from the tin box.

He was finished with the single papers by the time Keith handed him the small leather notebook to bag and tag. Gerry wondered what might be there that had so convinced the Professor of its uselessness but he didn't get a chance to have a look. After he'd entered the catalog info into the laptop and bagged the diary, it and the pile of bagged papers went into the large waterproof plastic container they used to keep any specimens clean and dry.

He only got a chance for a quick look at some of the diary pages when he was linking Keith's photographs to the database entries for each page but didn't have any time to read them properly. Only a few words caught his attention: dolls, nightmares, fights, and funeral.

It was those snatched words he was thinking about as he went outside to join the others in a meal as the light went from the sky over their campsite.

3

Keith couldn't sleep. The students' meal had been a mélange of beans and sausages, baloney and eggs, all the ingredients of which the two lads had managed to burn and the resultant mess, despite the attempts of several beers to wash it down, still lay like a brick in his stomach. For the past few hours he had been on his back in his bunk watching the shadows play on the tent.

He tried to forget the problems he'd left back in the city, tried to let his mind drift unfettered but he was no closer to dropping off than he had been when he first crawled into the sleeping bag.

To make matters worse he shared his tent with the Professor and although the older man was a friend and mentor, he also snored like a honking goose, each coming at irregular enough intervals that it came as a surprise every time. The stomach cramps, the noise and the press of his worries in his mind, meant rest was well-nigh impossible.

Around two a.m. he gave in to the inevitable and fought his way out of the sleeping bag. The Professor's snores missed a couple of beats then came back as strong as ever. Keith pulled on his boots and then left the tent to head into the cool night air. Although only July a frost is never far off in Newfoundland especially on clear nights such as this. Any thought of sleep was blown away in the breeze that chilled his cheeks and felt cold at the back of his throat when he took a deep breath. At least it gave him something different to think about.

There was no sound from the other small tent. He'd heard Doug and Bill chatting loudly until after midnight and the clink of beer bottles reminded him he needed to have a word with them about their motivation in the morning. For now, he had the night and the view across the pond all to himself. He walked over to the pickup and retrieved his heavy denim jacket from where it hung over the back of the driver's seat then went to look out over the black water of the pond.

There was no moon tonight but the sparkle of the stars out here in the wild more than made up for that. The full arc of the Milky Way hung like a majestic jewel overhead and the shattered image of it danced and capered on the jet-black surface of the pond. Keith breathed deep, ignoring the cold, trying to force thoughts of Joanna and reminders of his problem out of his mind. She wouldn't stay down though and her harsh words of the night before kept coming back to him, one word in particular he still couldn't handle.

"Pregnant?" he'd said. "How can you be pregnant?"

"It's your dick. You tell me."

He'd only been home for two minutes but two seconds after those words they were into a full-blown shouting match that blew up out of nowhere and showed no signs of abating any time soon. It ended with Keith walking out. His dramatic slamming of the door for effect lost its power when it bounced open again behind him but by then he was on his way downstairs, heading for a bar.

Beer helped, then rum helped more but the word, the P-word, wouldn't go away.

He stayed in the bar until Joanna would be at work on her nightshift at the hospital then he'd gone home, managed with the help of more booze to catch a few hours' sleep, then headed straight out to the University early to get this current show on the road. They'd been well on the way up the island by the time she would have come off shift. He still hadn't talked to her since the row and had no idea what he was going to say to her in any case.

I can't be a father. Not yet and maybe not ever. I'm having enough trouble being an adult.

He loved Joanna; he'd loved her from the first night they met when she was the one stitching the gash in his leg after the drunken hockey accident in the park.

"You should see my other scars," he'd said, which as a pick-up line was about as feeble as it got but the drink had been doing his talking for him. She saw something through the fog of booze though and she'd humored him when he asked for her phone number. The next day he was embarrassed but not too much to make the call.

They went for a Chinese meal and had a few drinks, he stayed sober, she kept humoring him and things grew from there. Two years later he was graduated and had gotten the research assistant's job working under the Professor in the faculty. As soon as steady checks came in they'd moved in together.

He was still drinking too much with his mates, playing too many risky games of hockey, still spending much of his spare time in the George Street bars, still buying too many new games for his console, still closer in mind to eighteen than his current twenty-three. He wasn't sure he wanted to change yet.

At least he'd quit smoking this past year at Joanna's insistence but now he couldn't have one, out here in the middle of nowhere with the nearest cigarette a good fifty kilometers away, he found he wanted one badly. The craving became so huge that he checked the pockets of his jacket to make sure he didn't have an old pack squirreled away for emergencies.

He didn't find a smoke but he did find his phone. He switched it on expecting that she'd have called him sometime that evening before her next shift but he had no missed calls and no text messages. He had some bars so there was a service even out here in the wilds. She still wasn't talking.

She's waiting for me to make the first move. I should call her. She'll be at work and might not pick up but I can leave a message. I can make things right.

The only thing to make things right would be to acknowledge the pregnancy, take his responsibility for it and face the future; parenthood, marriage, settling down, being careful with cash and a whole different way of life. He couldn't see any way out of it without being a complete bastard and he didn't want that. He also couldn't see any way into it that would make him happy.

He switched off the phone again, the call unmade.

Maybe a few days out here will clear my head, let me think it through.

He put the phone away in the inside pocket of his jacket and stood, trying once again to let the emptiness of the night and the twinkle of the stars fill him up. After a while he was forced to admit it wasn't working. Calm and sleep were as far away as ever and now even the cold stars had lost their appeal as the chill threatened to eat into him.

Maybe focusing on something else for a while will help.

He headed, not for his sleeping bag but for the work tent.

He got the generator running, switched on the heater and set off a brew of coffee, attached the laptop to the big battery pack they'd brought with them so it would keep its charge and tried to get lost in the day's finds.

He flicked quickly through the images of the loose papers. Stock orders, invoices and staff rolls were interesting enough in their way and the small details of day to day life in the past was a big part of what Keith's job was all about. The humdrum could wait until they were back in the lab in the city on a snowy winter's day in a snug office when there was plenty of free time available.

It had been obvious that the Professor was disturbed by the foreman's diary and the hesitation in the older man had piqued Keith's interest. A diary like that should have the Professor ecstatic at the find; he had been that way when they discovered the notebook.

So, what did he read that changed his mind?

Keith read the first page.

"The diary of Joseph Patrick Donnelly, begun this day of our Lord 23rd May, 1874.

"It seems I have been appointed foreman for this stage of our expedition, although why me, I am at a loss to say. Mayhap because I am one of only three of us here who can write more than my name and place of birth. Or mayhap it is the fact I know the work only too well from my time in Wales and I am all too

aware of the inherent dangers in being over eager to get to the
lode, if there is any lode to be found. We shall see. It is not as if
I have anywhere else to be.

"I will not write here of our journey to this point. It is a long
sad tale all too familiar to Irishmen, a tale of famine at home
and backbreaking work abroad. In my case the work involved
toiling in the dark wells of the deepest coal mine in Wales, a job
I would not wish on my worst enemy. But it paid for food and
shelter, which was the most I could hope for from it.

"It was a chance encounter in a bar in Swansea and hope of
a new start that led me here to this point. Even so if my Jenny
had not died of the black lung last year I might not have taken
the offer and still be down under the Welsh valley in the dark
with the coal even yet.

"My grief took everything I valued from me and left me a
broken man. Given the chance I took the boat from Liverpool
heading east to St. John's and then via several twists and turns
was led here at the prospect of rock that might yield treasure.
We shall have to see about that.

"But at least here I am my own man, sleeping under the sky
and the stars. It is a long way from the valleys and I left no one
there to tend Jenny's grave, even though I made her a promise
before she went to keep the flowers fresh.

"I will be back to her. I will keep my promise as soon as the
job is done here.

"We have got off to a good enough start. We found the site
yesterday after only two days of searching in the wilds. There is
no track to speak of from Buchans to here but we have broken the
ground now and there will be enough backward and forward,
at least in these early days, that the way will be marked clear
enough for the summer to come.

"The cabin and huts are going up quickly. By the end of
the week we should have our quarters, stores and outhouses
squared away and ready for the operation proper to begin. In
the meantime, I have made a survey of the rock face to find the
weak points where blasting might be most fruitful and give us
the best return for the outlay we have made on the powder.

"I had been worried before we made the trek here that we

had insufficient provisions at hand for a crew of this size. But although we might lack in vegetables we shall not want for much for the area fair teems with life. There is an abundance of meat in the form of trapped beaver and netted fish and we may even mayhap down a moose if one of us can shoot straight enough. With that, the flour and dry biscuits we have carted here and the profusion of local berries, we have enough to ensure we will not starve.

"It is only for several months in any case for we have to be away well before winter's grip; we all know we would not last a week here once the snow and ice comes down from the North.

"But it is not fear or apprehension I feel today; it is excitement. We are almost ready and there is a vein of silver deep in this rock. I would stake my life on it."

Keith paused and took a break while he fetched a mug of coffee.

He'd been right about one thing, reading the journal had taken his mind off his own problems. Even for the space of the short first entry he'd been sucked in to Donnelly's story, lost more than a century previously. It amazed Keith to think he might be reading the words in almost exactly the same spot where they were written so long ago. The sense of the interconnectedness of history, one of the things that had drawn him to this field in the first place, was almost palpable.

There was, however, nothing that should have bothered the Professor in the way it had but the old man had read farther, had spent several hours at it. Keith flicked a few pages ahead, slowly, trying to get the gist of the activity that had taken place here almost a century and a half ago. Joseph Donnelly was writing for himself only; the journal was not addressed to anyone else and it was obvious the man had come to Newfoundland to escape the private grief mentioned in the first page.

When it comes to escape I can relate.

In the early part of the journal at least, Keith still found nothing that would have discomforted the old professor. Donnelly detailed the early stages of the operation, building the dwelling quarters to a state where they could be lived in, having latrines dug and outhouses built and making a start on blasting their way into the rock. Then they began to mine and things got interesting.

Keith sipped at the coffee and returned to eighteen seventy-four with the miners.

It had not gone well.

"June 19th

"Damn this obdurate rock. I have had to send Murphy and Callaghan off by cart to fetch more pick-axes and shovels, for this stone shreds our gear as if it were little more than wet paper and resists all our efforts to delve into its secrets. They have taken both our ponies and most of what money we have left to us. God alone knows when, or even whether, they will return.

"In the meantime, we will have to make do with what we have at hand although at this rate we may have precious few tools left to us by this time next week. The men mutter and complain and I cannot say as I blame them much for it has been one bloody mess after another so far.

"The powder is all used up, our second shaft has come up devoid of a seam and, worse than that, wet, having filled in at the bottom in a deep pool that refuses to be drained. It might even be connected underground to our pond, in which case we will never get it empty.

"I have made the decision to concentrate on shaft one. We have reached a depth of thirty feet there and although it is dry it is hard going and the men can only work in short shifts in the cramped dark. Of course, conditions are nowhere near as bad as those faced half a mile and more deep in the Welsh coal but most of these men, unlike myself, have not been down in the well of darkness and they find little here to their liking.

"Outside in the huts where we have made our home, conditions are scarcely improved. Black flies plague us at every turn, swarms of them so thick they get in your hair, ears, nostrils, and mouth and the taste of them on your tongue is like acrid ash and shite. The only place you can get any kind of peace is in the huts but of necessity doors and shutters have to be kept closed to keep the flies out and by noon the heat has become so oppressive even the flies seem preferable.

"Pipe tobacco gives us some relief by keeping the worst of the insects at a distance but our supplies of the weed run low; another thing I added to Murphy and Callaghan's list when I sent them off.

"All of this expense means our coffers are almost empty and if we do not hit a seam of silver or gold, even copper or nickel would do, then the whole summer will have to be written off. If that becomes the case we will leave here penniless and destitute men with few prospects of surviving the winter to come no matter where we end up on this island and even less prospect of funding any desired passage back across the ocean to hearth and home.

"The morale of the men is variable, swinging from hope to despair in equal measures. There has, of late, been grumbling of discontent with the nature of their victuals. Any fish we have caught from the dark pond have tasted sour, like vinegar in our mouths and the single beaver we managed to entrap was little more than fat and gristle that made an almost inedible stew. We survive, for now, on thin gruel, berries and dry biscuits. Matters are not helped by the fact the second to last barrel of ale has been cracked open and our uisque supply is dwindling visibly.

"The Cork man, Padhraig Malone, has been the main instigator of the most recent spate of complaints. Malone has previous experience leading men as a low-ranking officer in the army in India and acts like he is the most important among the lot of us. I do believe he has not forgiven the others for choosing me as their foreman and he now opposes me at every turn, probing for any weakness he might be able to exploit to his advantage.

"Tonight's little mummery was all a result of his

suggestion of a means to raise the men's sprits. I agreed to it only because I sensed the mood of the men at the end of the shift and I am not sure whether the crew's morale is an iota improved as a result. But it will make a grand tale for the children in our dotage if it works.

"It all began when Malone suggested a source of our problems and his plan for their resolution. Miners are on the whole a superstitious lot and we have all heard the old tales of knockers and kobolds, gnomes and specters, denizens of the dark jealously guarding their treasures. Some of us even have experience of dark things met in darker places. We do not normally speak of them unless we are in our cups.

"But tonight, Malone brought such matters out into the light for us all to consider. What he promised is an age-old ceremony, ancient even before the blessed Saint Patrick drove the snakes from the land. It is one I have seen done before, always in the auld country, never here in this New Found Land. But the big man is most persuasive and he had gauged the mood of the men well enough to know they would go along with him on the matter. His hope was I would say no and give him an opportunity to question my authority. I was not inclined to give him the satisfaction.

"'We're here,' he said. 'Why shouldn't the Wee Folk be here too?'

"Nobody had an answer to naysay him and I knew better than to argue the toss, so the performance began.

"Malone led the proceedings, beginning with entreaties to St. Patrick, St. Michael, the Mother Mary, the Holy Ghost, and all of the heavenly hosts. He sang, he prayed, he preached, and by the Lord it was as if he had a touch of fire and brimstone in him. I will not begrudge him it for it was as fine a performance as you'll see on any stage in London or Dublin.

"Then he had a belly of ale and of uisque before moving on to older, more arcane specters at our feast. His tone softened and became almost pleading, calling on the Sidhe, the Hound, Finn, and a whole pantheon of fae folk, asking them for help, promising them fealty and any manner of tributes in they would only look kindly on our endeavors.

"By this time Malone was worked into a fine old froth and the rest of the men were infected with the fervor of it, stamping their feet and hollering along with every prayer, every snatch of song and call for aid.

"The performance ended with a long rendition in Gaelic of an old song, one we all know from our mother's knee and there was scarcely a dry eye in the house as we raised our voices in brotherhood and friendship.

"And once it was done there was nothing for it but for us all to troop out into the dark and down to the dark pool at the bottom of shaft two. Malone made another plea to the Wee Folk and we poured our drinks down into the water, a libation and our offering in exchange for their help.

"Malone looked at me and smiled but there was little joy in it, only cunning and guile, for I do believe he thinks he has got one over on me. Time will tell. By now most of us felt either drunk or weary and ready to retire to bed so we all, slowly, one by one, walked away back to camp, hopeful of a better tomorrow.

"Hope is about all we have now."

Is that it?

Keith looked up from the screen. He knew the Professor had been raised a Baptist and although he didn't seem particularly devout, was it this peculiarly Irish mixture of Catholicism and ancient mysticism that had led him to dismiss the diary completely?

Surely there must be more to it than that?

Keith was about to head farther into the diary when he absent-mindedly picked up his mug and noticed the coffee had gone cold. He checked the clock in the bottom corner of the laptop. It was already past three a.m. and he needed to be bright eyed and bushy tailed in the morning, or at least as close to it as he was going to get now.

His head was still full of the story from the journal. He'd been lost in it, like reading a good book, smelling their pipe smoke, tasting their whiskey, hearing their songs, but they'd still be there between the pages in the morning. He reluctantly powered the computer down, switched off the propane heater, and went back out into the night, heading, finally, for his sleeping bag.

As he left the tent he heard a splash over at the pond, not too loud but none too quiet either. He realized he hadn't seen any sign of life, not even a bird, since their arrival but there were beaver all over the island, moose and bear too. There were even wolves in scattered isolation but he had never heard of anyone being attacked by one, especially so close to a camp and besides the splash had been too innocuous to have been made by any large predator. The noise had him intrigued enough to step over to the pickup and look over the hood toward the black still waters of the pond.

There was nothing to see, only ripples fracturing the reflection of the arc of the Milky Way above. He stood there for over a minute waiting for a recurrence of the noise in the water but none came. As he finally turned away he thought he caught a flash of color at the edge of the pond, green, like Joanna's eyes but when he looked again there was only the dark and shifting shadows.

He made his way to the tent and, finally tired, kicked off his boots and climbed into the sleeping bag. He drifted away into the cozy warmth with thoughts of Irish miners in his head and as he was going under he heard them singing their slow and mournful songs of the auld country.

Bring back, oh bring back, oh bring back my bonnie to me, to me.

4

Gerry made sure he was first up in the morning so he could take control of the camping stove for breakfast. He couldn't stomach another burnt offering like last night's pitiful excuse for supper. That and the fact Doug farted like an incontinent camel most of the night meant he was happy to be outside in clearer air, even if the morning felt more like January than July. He warmed up quickly enough once he got the stove going and prepared what he hoped was enough breakfast and coffee for the five of them.

He needn't have worried about volume. The grudging approval he got from Doug and Bill when he served up eggs, bacon, toast and coffee without a burnt item among them made up for the fact that both Keith and the Professor ate perfunctorily, each seemingly lost in their own thoughts. The coffee disappeared fast enough though and they were well down the second pot by the time the food was gone.

While Keith was quiet and preoccupied, the Professor perked up after the clearing up of the breakfast dishes was over and done.

"Gerry, you're with me this morning, over at the rock looking for the workings. According to the diary there are two shafts there somewhere and today we're going to find them. Keith, you take these other two slackers and check out those ruined buildings we saw yesterday. See what you can find of the camp. It didn't look like there's going to be much left but you never know."

Gerry got the camp stove stowed away, made sure he had his camera, tablet, a flashlight, and his notebook in his satchel and followed the Professor out of the camp. He wasn't able to keep a smirk from his face as he passed Doug and Bill; they all knew Gerry had got the day's prime gig. He mouthed one word at them but he enjoyed every bit of it.

Slackers.

He followed the Professor over to the rock face. This early in the day the sun fell full on the rock, or it would have done on a better morning. Thin, ineffectual sunlight peeked through low slow-moving cloud, not enough to bring any warmth and Gerry was thankful he'd worn his jacket. As they stepped off the flat area of rock and gravel where they'd camped, the ground was soggy underfoot but it firmed as they went up the slight incline to reach the rock face itself.

The dome of rock loomed high over them, almost vertical and dark against the sky. Patchy fingers of sparse vegetation were outlined against the skyline but for the most part the rock face looked bare and forbidding.

"Why would anyone even think of mining here?" Gerry said.

"What we have here is an igneous intrusion," the Professor said. "These rocks are often shot through with faults and where you get faults, you get accumulations of minerals, precious metals, even gemstones. Trust me, these chaps knew what they were after well enough. Whether they found it or not is a matter we shall have to investigate at some length. But first things first. Let's find the shafts before we start wondering what was down in them."

At first glance there was no sign anyone but the two of them had ever been here; the base of the rock was covered in a matted mass of thick shrubbery. Tangled, dead branches intermingled with the green shoots of new growth, ash and birch and juniper all growing and intertwining together in a dense carpet. Gerry looked both ways along the stone face; it did not look any more encouraging in either direction.

The Professor clapped him on the shoulder.

"The shafts are here, lad. We've got the paperwork to prove it. Now let's do the legwork."

It didn't take long for the Professor to be proved right. Gerry almost tripped over a length of rusted iron rail and following it toward the rock face led them straight to the mouth of two distinct shafts almost completely obscured by mostly dead, matted shrubbery, hard to see until you were right up next to them. They were obvious now Gerry could see them up close, although from the earlier, lower, angle they'd only looked like deeper shadows under a slight overhang.

Even then it didn't prove easy to get at them. It took Gerry and the Professor almost fifteen minutes to clear the vegetation; it had taken deep hold in a softer patch of soil around the mouths of the mines.

Gerry soon wished he'd remembered to bring gloves. The Professor had a pair made of old soft leather, perfect for the job and the older man was able to tug and pull at the vegetation with gusto. Gerry wasn't so lucky, for although there were no thorns as such, there were plenty of splinters in the dead wood. He had to pull two deep ones out from his left hand with his teeth, raising tiny globes of blood both times. On top of that, stinging sap in the sparse branches of newer growth left him with hot angry patches of livid red on the palms and backs of both hands before the job was done. Finally, they cleared enough to allow them passage to both of the dark tunnels.

While the Professor studied the mouths of the shafts, Gerry sucked at the still bleeding puncture wounds on his hands. They looked clean enough and the flow of blood stopped when he stopped sucking.

Looks like I'll live.

"What do you think, lad?" the Professor asked as they stood in front of the shafts, like dark eyes staring back at them, almost daring them to enter. "Door number one or door number two? How's your luck?"

Gerry got his flashlight from his satchel and checked it was working before he stepped forward. The left-hand cave looked less defined in shape whereas the right was an almost perfect semi-circle. It was irrational he knew but it looked more inviting.

"Let's try the right," he said.

"Lay on then, MacDuff," the Professor replied, "and don't spare the horses."

They went right, heading into the quiet dark.

They had only stepped five feet inside when the shaft narrowed considerably. Gerry stood six feet tall and his hair brushed the roof; if he stretched out his hands he could touch the rough walls on either side. He'd never knowingly suffered from claustrophobia but right now all of his senses were telling him to back away lest he get trapped like a cork in a bottle. The flashlight didn't penetrate far enough to show if the cave got any narrower; Gerry wasn't sure he wanted to know.

He looked back and saw the Professor outlined in the cave mouth.

"I've got your back, lad," the man said. "You'll be fine. The diary says they mined in both shafts so there'll be room to get in and out. Watch where you're putting your feet and take it nice and slow."

They moved inside in single file with Gerry going first. He was pleased to see it was no longer narrowing, although it got dark within a few paces as they lost the benefit of the light seeping in from outside.

It wasn't too far in before the passage took a downward slope and Gerry had to take smaller, more careful steps, for his flashlight only illuminated some six to eight feet in front of him; anything beyond was black and quiet.

The smallest noises were amplified now, echoing around them, tiny whispers encouraging him to hurry, to go deeper. Gerry almost smiled; he hadn't been spooked by the dark since he was a kid but if it were ever to happen, surely it would be in a place like this?

He swung his light back and forth but there was nothing to see but the rough walls, scarred in linear strokes where the workings had left their mark. The rock faces looked uniformly gray and slightly damp although there was no sign of any moss or lichen. The passageway underfoot was similarly uniform, being hard, pitted rock, wet but not slippery, although the slope was more accentuated now they were deeper.

His flashlight beam picked out something different on the left-side wall and he stopped briefly for a closer look. It was a name and a date, *Pat Malone, 3rd July, 1874,* crudely carved into the rock. Gerry ran his fingers over it and felt the slight indentation where the tool, whether it was knife or chisel, had etched into stone.

The Professor Came to Gerry's shoulder to see why he'd stopped.

"Malone. He's mentioned in the diary," he said. "We're definitely on the right track, lad. Let's see what's waiting down below, shall we?"

They went down, slowly and carefully, for several minutes. The air felt cold against his face and took on a dampness Gerry tasted in his throat. It had a strong tang to it, acrid, like sniffing a bottle of malt vinegar, with an undercurrent of burnt oil. He stopped so suddenly the Professor walked into him and almost toppled them both.

"Sorry," Gerry said. "But I don't think there's anything to see here, Professor and it smells damp and bad."

"A bit farther, lad," the Professor said. "I think this must be number two shaft. The diary said it suffered from being wet."

It wasn't the wet Gerry was thinking about as they started down again. It was the other words he'd noted while reading the scanned papers, nightmares and funeral.

They hit bottom a minute or so later. This time Gerry gave the Professor plenty of warning that he needed to stop and with good cause, for if they tumbled forward, they'd both have gone headfirst into a still, dark pool of unknown depth.

It lay under the light of the flashlight, flat calm and reflective, a black mirror set in the bottom of the mine. They found their first sign since Malone's graffiti that someone else had been there. Two whiskey bottles sat at Gerry's feet on the edge of the pool. He bent and was about to pick up the nearest bottle to his toes when the Professor stopped him.

"Wait. We need to document everything on the way in. Photographs first."

Gerry was close enough to get a good look at the bottle. The label was faint and peeling but was clear enough, Irish, from the Bushmills distillery, County Antrim. The date on the bottle said it was bottled in 1859.

The Professor made notes of where the bottles had been found and Gerry took a series of pictures of them in situ, moving around the pool as much as he could to get different angles.

The flash from the camera sent small ripples running across the surface of the black pool, as if the light itself was causing a vibration. The whispering echoes as their feet slapped on wet rock took on a hissing, sibilant tone. It grated on Gerry's nerves and he hurried to bag and tag the whiskey bottles once the Professor was satisfied they'd taken enough photos.

The Professor picked up on Gerry's unease. "Are you okay, lad?"

Gerry laughed but the echoes rising as a result were harsh and cold and brought an involuntary shiver, making him long for the relative warmth up in the open air.

"I might not be claustrophobic, Professor but this place gives me the willies."

The Professor's laughter echoed even louder, even colder in the small chamber.

"It's just the damp. Let's get packed up here and see if Keith's got some coffee brewing."

As he packed the bottles away Gerry saw the second bottle still had a cork in it and an inch of liquid in the bottom, although in the beam of the flashlight it looked thick, viscous and black, too oily to be drinkable. He felt it slosh from side to side in his backpack as they turned away from the pool and began their slow climb up out of the dark.

It's been down here since before my great grandfather was born.

The next thought came unbidden. He wasn't much of a liquor drinker but suddenly and out of nowhere, he needed to know.

I wonder what it tastes like?

5

Doug and Bill were obviously not interested in the day ahead of them.

"Look, are you here to work, or are you here to fuck around?" Keith said when he found them having a beer at the side of the pond. "Either way, make your mind up."

That got them moving, for now but Keith knew he'd be chivvying them along all morning to get the smallest things done. In some ways Keith could hardly blame them after all, he wasn't really interested himself, not after last night's broken sleep. He had managed to nod off after slipping back into the sleeping bag but his dreams were troubled and fractured flashes of emerald, working a rock face with a pick in the dark, drowning in deep, cold, black water, and eyes, always green, staring at him. He'd woken in a sweat to the sound of the Professor honking furiously.

The first thing he'd done after the Professor got up and left the tent was to try to call Joanna again. She'd be arriving home from her shift about then but although he got a signal, she didn't answer the phone and when her voicemail message kicked in he didn't reply. Whatever he had to say, she deserved to hear it first-hand.

Now, after breakfast, he wanted to try again, even though she'd probably be in bed by now but the two students were apt to slack off given the slightest opportunity and he respected the Professor and the job too much to allow them the luxury of goofing off.

He looked over toward the rock face. The Professor and Gerry were clearing away vegetation around a particular spot and didn't look like they needed any help with it.

The old camp it is then.

Keith turned back and motioned to the other two students to follow him, heading south into the denser patches of shrubs and stunted trees. His feet squelched wetly with every step, even as he did his best to avoid the dark puddles hiding in wait for any unwary steps and he was grateful for his stout boots.

One of the lads, Bill, was only wearing Converse trainers and stood, soaked ankle deep in cold cloying mud after only two minutes in the undergrowth. They'd only reached the remains of the outhouse Keith and the Professor had found the day before and hadn't even begun to explore the rougher terrain beyond that.

"This sucks," Bill said, loud enough for all three of them to hear.

"It's going to get much worse before it gets better," Keith replied and grinned at the grimace he got back in reply.

His day was slowly improving.

They found the spot where the Professor tripped over the tin box after only a few minutes more searching; the rectangular depression in the muddy ground was unmistakable and obviously recent.

Keith photographed the wet hole from several angles.

"This is important," he said, tapping the camera. "We need to document everything on the way in. So, if you spot anything you think is relevant, shout and don't touch. Clear?"

He made sure they understood. Mollycoddling them like kindergarten kids was going to make them sullen but it looked like it was the only way to make sure they didn't fuck this whole trip up with a slapdash approach.

Keith had another look around before leading the students deeper into the foliage. He was trying to remember where they'd stood when they noticed the remains of the sheds the day before. Then he caught a glimpse of a clearer area through the foliage that looked familiar and headed in that direction. The two younger men thrashed and splashed and complained their way along behind him.

The first thing he noticed as he approached the clearing was the twig figures. Everywhere he turned there were more of them, scattered in the branches of the mountain-ash bushes in various poses, sitting, standing or draped over twigs. None more than a foot tall, all were delicately made with fresh foliage starting to yellow at the edges. They looked to be the work of a craftsman of considerable skill.

But what are they doing all the way out here in the middle of nowhere? Who put them here?

None of the figures, thankfully for Keith's state of mind, had green staring eyes. The trick of the light yesterday had been just that and Keith tried to convince himself these were no more than an amusement put in place by someone, most probably a gifted child with too much time on their hands on a boring family camping trip. From the yellowing on the leaves it looked like they'd been made recently, sometime in the past week or so.

"These are creepy as fuck," Doug said and Keith had to agree. There was something decidedly off-putting about the ranks of figures, apparently ready to spring into action the moment your back was turned.

"Minds on the job, guys," Keith said. "These are too recent to be of any concern to us. We're looking for Irish miners, not kids making dolls."

He moved deeper into the rough, almost dense, thickets, still heading south, his gaze fixed on the more open ground he could see only several meters ahead now. He pushed through thicker, livelier, branches; they whipped against his arms and legs and threatened to slap hard at his face. The black flies swarmed all around, flying into his eyes, mouth and ears and he tasted one on his tongue, *acrid, like shite,* then finally he stepped through the foliage and into a wide, roughly circular area, obviously cleared by someone at some time in the past.

How it had stayed cleared was going to be a matter for some debate, for the ground was gray, gravel covered and with not a hint of a weed or flower in its twenty meter or so diameter. Keith had more on his mind. The Professor had said he'd be surprised if there was much left to find of the camp.

Well, he's going to be surprised then.

There had been three wooden structures in the clearing at
one time, two of which were tumbled in on themselves. One of
those two had obviously burned to the ground and was little more
than ash and charred wood and the other was an irregular pile of
rotting timber that might yield better finds under the wood.

It was the third structure that was the big surprise. It was
much larger than the others, almost twenty feet long at its longest
and more of a log cabin than a hut. It had stood the test of time
much better.

It was obviously rough-hewn and put up with little finesse
in the making but it had proved sturdy enough to withstand a
hundred and forty and more Newfoundland winters. There were
houses all across the island that wouldn't last half as long as this
one had.

The whole building still stood, mostly, although the wood-
shingled roof had badly slumped down at the southern end,
many of the shingles were missing and the main door hung
lopsided in the frame, held there by what strength was left in a
single rusted hinge.

Keith motioned Doug and Bill to stay back as he walked
around the perimeter of the clearing, taking photographs at
intervals, obtaining the information required for the software
they had back in the city to build a 3-D model of the entire site.

He had to wipe the lens clear every few seconds. There were
still plenty of the black flies here and not for the first time on the
trip Keith wished he had a smoke, remembering the passage he'd
read in the foreman's diary the night before about the efficacy of
tobacco against the menace.

Keeping on the move was the best way to avoid the flies so
after one more close-up of the front of the cabin, he headed for
the doorway.

Slowly, carefully, he stepped up onto the small porch, testing
it to make sure it would take his weight. An alarming creak
echoed loudly around the clearing and there was a lot of spring
in the old wood, like standing on a trampoline bed but it felt solid
enough to take his weight. He stepped up and peered in through
the half-open door not daring to touch it yet for fear that if it fell

the whole building might follow.

"Can we come forward, Keith?" one of the lads behind shouted and he waved them on.

"Head on over. But don't come inside, or even up onto this porch, until I give the all clear. And don't touch anything."

His view into the large room beyond was partially obscured by the half-open door but he saw beds along the right-side wall, in two tiers, with blankets hanging off them. An old iron stove dominated the far end of the room, with several empty chairs gathered around it. The whole place was remarkably clear of dust or dirt and there was no sign of rot, moss or mildew. If it had not been for the broken door and sagging roof it would almost have looked as if the place was waiting for the mining party to return from its shift.

The Professor is going to love this.

A slight breeze got up and the door creaked on its hinges. Keith smelled something acrid and tangy, like vinegar and burnt oil catching at the back of his throat and making him cough, then the breeze took it away as quickly as it had come.

Doug and Bill had come up close behind him, both at least having the good sense to do as they were told and keep their weight off the porch.

"Are we going in?" Bill said and for the first time on the trip Keith heard excitement if not exactly enthusiasm in the youth's voice.

We might make an archaeologist out of him yet.

Again, he didn't blame the lad for any excitement. He felt it too, on the verge of a step into the unknown, with possible historical treasures to be found on the other side of the door.

"Wait until I say it's safe, okay?" he said. Both the youths nodded in agreement then Keith turned to the door and as gently as he could manage, pushed it open. The old hinge creaked alarmingly and the door slumped an inch toward the jamb but it held and swung inward slowly, groaning all the way.

Keith stood in the doorway and took pictures of the bunks and the stove before venturing inside. It was only then he spotted the table, laid for supper... and the six figures sitting around it, seemingly engaged in conversation.

His heart fluttered like a small bird taking flight and breath came in short gasps. His head told him to run but his legs weren't listening. It was a few seconds before he calmed enough to notice the yellow-edged foliage and realized he was not looking at human bodies and certainly not any kind of specters.

Whoever had been busy out in the scrub making the tiny doll-like figures had been even busier in here. Six full-size almost life like mannequins sat, arranged around the wooden table in naturalistic poses, made by someone with real skill and craftsmanship. They all looked male and, somehow, although none of them were clothed, they all looked like miners relaxing after a hard day at the face. Clay mugs and tin plates sat on the table, knives and forks arranged as if a meal had recently been taken but it was the sculptures themselves that caught the eye and would not let go.

Here was a hand with a pipe in it being raised for a smoke but stopped in mid-sentence, there was a leg casually draped over the ankle of the other. One of the figurines had its head back, mouth open and Keith could almost hear the raucous laughter echoing around the room. Again, as in the figures outside, the foliage, the meat on the wooden bones of the structures, looked green and fresh, starting to tinge yellow at the edges.

Keith had no idea how long it might have taken to make such things but he was pretty sure it was a task beyond a bored kid on a family camping holiday.

What the hell is this?

The floor felt sound enough underfoot so Keith motioned to the other two it was safe for them to come forward.

"And prepare yourselves. There's some weird shit in here. If you thought the dolls in the trees were creepy, you're going to love this."

He saw their eyes go wide when they took note of the seated figures, their gaze locked on the table, making them incapable of looking away. Keith had to raise his voice to get their attention.

"It's just some bigger versions of those dolls," he said. "That's all. I know it looks peculiar but it's some artist out here getting away from it all. It has to be."

At least I hope that's all it is.

He had to get the lads to work, give them something to do, otherwise they'd stand and stare at the sculptures all morning.

"Doug, you take the beds. Slowly, remember. Check there's nothing between the sheets or under the pillows, or even under the beds themselves. And if you do find anything, don't touch it. Holler so I can photograph it in situ. The same applies to you, Bill, take everything steady. You take the stove and surrounding area. It looks like there's a cupboard or a pantry or something behind it. Don't touch it until I get over there. I'm going to take photos of our family group here first. The Professor will want these."

Although I'm not sure he'll understand them any more than I do.

Keith turned his attention back to the wooden mannequins. It was proving hard to look at anything else. He circled the table taking photographs from every angle and trying to avoid looking too long at the largest figure seated at the head of the table, a broad-shouldered man with a huge bushy green beard and dark eye sockets following Keith with their gaze wherever he moved to.

He eventually noticed something else too. Although the door lay partially open and the shutters across the glass-free windows were not closed, there were no black flies inside the cabin. There was a definite feeling of death and silence, almost funereal.

Keith found he was subconsciously keeping movement to a minimum and keeping his voice low when he spoke, as if doing so might violate some unspoken rule, or offend some unseen overseer of this tableau.

He circled the table twice, taking forty or more photographs and still the big bearded man at the end of the table stared mutely at him.

Is this supposed to be the Foreman? Is that what we have here? Is this a monument to the lost miners?

He was at a loss to explain it and hoped to leave it to the Professor's superior experience.

Bill called him over to the other side of the room when he stopped snapping photographs.

"There's definitely a door here. Pantry maybe?"

Keith stepped over and opened it gingerly. Once again, the sound of creaking hinges echoed around them but the door opened smoothly enough to reveal a small storage area inside.

There was no sign any rodents had gotten into the pantry, another small miracle on this island in an old building. Most of the foodstuffs were long past being edible although there was a sack of rough milled oats spilling onto the shelf that looked like they'd still make a good gruel. There was a tin of tea, now turned to dry black powder, alongside a sack of what had once been biscuits but were now crumbled, green and black crumbs. Something long and almost rectangular that had probably been cheese was now a colony of something else entirely. Surprisingly none of it smelled rank and there was no hint of the black mold Keith expected to see.

The only other thing of note any of them found in the whole room was a long-stemmed clay pipe on the table. The bowl was packed with some kind of seeds. Keith photographed, bagged and tagged it and stowed it away in his camera bag over his shoulder before leading the other two out into the sunlight.

"What about the plates, cups and cutlery?" Bill said. Keith noted the lad purposefully avoided looking at the table and the seated figures.

Keith kept his eyes on the youth as he replied. The sculptures demanded attention and Keith was afraid if he stayed there long enough he might never leave, might join them at the table as the vegetation grew around and inside him

He pushed the thought away fast.

God, I need a smoke.

"I've got the photos," he said. "That's enough for now and will keep the Professor happy for a while. We'll come back later with a box to stow the tableware in."

He closed the door softly behind them as they left.

It felt like the right and proper thing to do.

6

Gerry walked behind the Professor for the descent into shaft one. He wasn't yet sure if it was a good or a bad thing; it meant the Professor would be first to get into trouble if there was any trouble to be had. It also meant all Gerry could see was the older man's back and the dry rock underfoot as he kept his own flashlight lowered to check where he stepped.

He'd thought their time in the other shaft might have been enough excitement for the morning, given they had finds to bag and tag. Having come this far the Professor wasn't about to leave so quickly, despite his earlier statement about coffee.

"A quick look," he said. "We'll get in and out. If we find anything we'll leave it and come back later. Promise."

So, Gerry followed.

At least it was drier here, although it was far from being a quick walk in and out. They had already gone deeper than they had managed in shaft two and the air thickened, almost cloying in Gerry's throat and nostrils. The only sound was their slightly labored breathing and the pad of feet on rock.

Also, for Gerry's ears only, the slight, almost imperceptible, sloshing of the liquid inside the whiskey bottle in his satchel kept reminding him it was there. Ever since he'd picked up the bottle he'd thought of little else but the taste of it. It worried away at his mind, tempting him, confusing him. Gerry liked a drink and sometimes he liked a lot of drink but usually beer, occasionally rum and only at weekends with pals in noisy bars and clubs. The idea of drinking whiskey and drinking it alone had never even occurred to him until now but it was the only thing he could think of as he followed the Professor down into the dark.

Is this how an alcoholic starts?

He pushed the thought away and tried to concentrate on putting one foot after the other. This shaft wasn't as steep as the previous one but the ground underfoot was more grooved and pitted and he didn't fancy twisting an ankle or worse, breaking a leg, down here.

The air got thicker still and again tasted of burned oil and vinegar, so much so Gerry covered his mouth with his hand and tried to breathe shallowly.

A wee drink would help with that.

It wasn't his own voice in his head but a high, soft, Irish-accentuated one that went quiet when the Professor spoke over his shoulder.

"It's a bit rank, isn't it? A few meters more then we'll give up and come back later with some masks and better lights. Deal?"

"Deal," Gerry replied, then closed his mouth fast as the taste tickled his tonsils and brought on a gag reflex.

Whiskey's good for a tickle in the throat.

The small, strangely Irish, voice at the back of his mind was persistent but he pushed it away again.

He was about to remind the Professor of his promise to turn back when the older man spoke.

"Hold up. We've got something here."

He shuffled to one side to allow Gerry to come up beside him. They both shone their flashlights down the tunnel ahead. At first Gerry thought it was matted vegetation blocking the way, tree roots having come down from somewhere high above, burrowing through cracks in the rocks to fill the spaces below.

Then he saw a face, cunningly wrought from large twigs, pieces of root and withered brown leaves, sculpted to give every impression of a man screaming in agony. Once he'd noticed that it was like looking at one of those trick holograms when it suddenly comes into focus. He saw faces and torsos and limbs, all twisted and entwined in a roiling, screaming mass. The grotesque sculpture in wood and root and leaf filled the whole tunnel from floor to roof, wall to wall. There would be no way to pass without chopping their way through with an axe and even then, it looked like a task far more work than the weekend they had available to them.

"What is it, Professor?" Gerry asked. He noticed the older man's flashlight was shaking as if his hand was trembling but the voice that replied was steady enough.

"It's a remarkable piece of sculpture," the Professor said. "But it's far too recent to be of much interest to us. Look, some of the foliage is still fresh."

Everything appeared rather flat and almost monochrome in the torchlight but Gerry saw the Professor was right. Some of the leaves were green with only a hint of yellow at the edges.

"Who would want to do this all the way out here where nobody would ever see it?" Gerry asked.

The Professor merely shrugged.

"Whoever it was, it's going to cause us a deal of bother if we want to study the rest of the shaft. Take some pictures anyway. May as well document it while we're here."

When Gerry focused the camera on the figures it brought them into even sharper relief and he marveled at the skill of the sculptor, while all the time wondering what madness might have driven them to hide their genius in a dark hole in a forgotten corner of the wild.

After Gerry took a dozen or so photographs the Professor had seen enough.

"Come on. Let's head back. We can do nothing here now without tools and more manpower."

And a lot of time we don't have.

Gerry thought it but didn't say it. Whoever had put this sculpture down here in the shaft had meant to do it and they'd meant to block the access to the deeper levels. What bothered Gerry as he turned to follow the Professor was why.

What didn't they want us to see? Or is the sculpture a statement in itself?

As they climbed back out Gerry realized the Professor intended to come back, to somehow remove the obstructive wood sculpture from the tunnel. The mere thought of it brought the little voice again at the back of his mind.

Best if you have a drink. You know you want to. There could be some nasty work in the dark ahead. A wee stiffener will do you the world of good.

Gerry didn't pause to wonder why, or how, an Irishman had gotten into his head. He was too busy thinking about the whiskey and what it might taste like.

Gerry followed the Professor back out of the shaft. They didn't speak but the climb back up proved easier than he had feared and they were soon at the mouth of the shaft, blinking in the thin watery sunlight. They immediately had to swat away a swarm of black flies. They hurried back toward the relative safety of the camp, having to wave their arms like demented dancers the whole way.

Keith, Doug and Bill were already in the work tent, with the flap firmly closed against the black fly invasion. A pot of coffee had been brewed and Keith was working on the laptop explaining something to the other two.

"Anything?" Keith asked.

The Professor sounded disappointed.

"A couple of small finds but nothing major. One wet shaft and one blocked with vegetation. Nothing we'll be able to do anything about before going home. How about you?"

"Better news than yours. We found the camp, Professor," Keith said over his shoulder as he made sure the tent flap was firmly closed again. "And it's everything you hoped for."

The older man grew animated; the look on his face like a kid seeing his pile of Christmas presents.

"There's something left of it? Something we can document?"

Keith grinned.

"Better than that. There's a whole cabin still standing. I've got the pictures."

"Blow the pictures. Take me to it."

Keith smiled.

"I thought that's what you'd say." He turned back to the three students.

"Doug, Bill, you two get the photos cataloged in the database and bag and tag the pipe properly. Then help Gerry with anything that he's got. Okay?"

"Pipe?" the Professor said and Keith laughed.

"Yep. There's a pipe. But if you want to see that, you can't see the camp."

The Professor laughed back at him. Gerry saw that all of the older man's earlier apprehension when faced by the sculpture in the shaft had vanished with the prospect of seeing what Keith had found.

"Lead the way," the Professor said. He followed Keith back out of the tent and the three younger men were left alone.

Gerry wished he had gone with the older two men. Bill and Doug were preoccupied, as it looked like there had been a lot of pictures taken of whatever they had found and they were hogging the laptop.

"Can I have a look?" Gerry asked.

"No," Doug replied bluntly and Gerry realized he was being punished for his earlier comment.

Slackers.

He mouthed it again, behind their backs but it made him feel better anyway. He sat down on one of the camp chairs with a mug of coffee in his hand, waiting his turn at the laptop.

The little Irish voice came back, even more insistent now that Gerry had nothing else to occupy his thoughts.

It goes well with coffee. A wee drop out of the bottle and nobody will ever know.

It felt like he had someone inside his head, or at his ear at least, an imp on his shoulder egging him on to dark deeds without the corresponding angel on the other side to balance him out. Gerry knew the voice should be ignored, knew he'd be tampering with a find and it would probably get him booted off the course. Equally, he wanted the same thing the voice wanted, felt it in his blood, in his bones, a deep-seated need not to be denied.

He made sure Bill and Doug were preoccupied, got the old whiskey bottle out of his satchel and without removing it from its plastic bag, uncorked it and dripped two thick droplets of the liquor into his coffee mug. By the time Doug turned far enough away from the laptop to be able to see him, Gerry already had the cork back in the bottle and the bag closed, making it look like he'd removed the specimen from his satchel in preparation for cataloging it.

The old liquor hadn't left any oily residue on top of the coffee he could see and when he sniffed it, he only smelled the usual bitter tang of the brew but Gerry stirred the hot liquid gingerly with his index finger first before taking a sip.

He almost cried out in joy at the sheer pleasure of it. It felt like the top of his head was going to lift off and a hot, toasty fire spread down his throat, into his stomach and through his whole body; he felt he had become some kind of walking radiator. The Irish voice was gleeful.

That's the right stuff, sure enough.

Gerry had to agree.

Go on, get some more down you. It'll put hairs on your chest, boyo.

He took to the rest of the drink with gusto.

7

Keith could hardly keep up with the Professor as they strode south towards the miners' campsite. Even the swarms of black flies couldn't dent the old man's enthusiasm but he was brought up short when he saw the small mannequins in the branches of the trees.

"I know you didn't put these here. Have you seen anybody around?"

Keith shook his head.

"They seem to be everywhere."

"And not only here. There's more down in the main mine shaft."

"More like these?"

"No, bigger. Much bigger."

Keith nodded.

"I was hoping you weren't going to say that."

The Professor went deathly still and quiet when they entered the old cabin and he saw the sculpted wood figures around the table.

"The whole bloody site's compromised, Keith," he said. "Somebody got here before us."

Keith stood and listened while the Professor detailed the full extent of the sculpture he and Gerry had found in the main shaft.

"I don't know why but it looks like there's been months of work for somebody to set this up. I don't think it's for our benefit. We haven't told anybody we were coming."

"I agree. It looks like a coincidence to me too. What does it mean, though?" Keith asked.

"I don't know and I don't care. It's some kind of art instillation project, I expect and if I find out it's by someone from a faculty back at Memorial in St Johns, then heads will roll."

Professor's next question came out of left field.

"Have you read the diary pages yet?"

"Not all of it. Only the first couple of weeks' entries and even then, I was mostly skimming my way through it."

"You should read it all and especially the pages near the end in the light of what we're seeing on site here. I thought I was the only one to read it since it was originally put in the tin box. But now I'm not so sure."

The older man wouldn't elaborate and in fact quickly lost all interest in the remains of the miners' camp. It wasn't like the Professor and his sudden indifference had Keith at a loss to explain it after his enthusiasm of the day before.

They walked back to their own campsite in silence, quickly, trying to avoid the flies. Neither of them mentioned the rows of mannequins in the trees providing an honor guard for their exit.

They arrived back in the work tent to find Gerry slumped in a camp chair and Bill and Doug standing over him as if unsure what to do about it.

"What's wrong with him?" the Professor said.

"We don't know," Bill replied. "One minute he was drinking coffee and was fine then when we turned around..."

Gerry slumped into what would be a long slow slide off his chair toward the ground. Keith was first to move. He strode forward, got Gerry upright again and lifted his head. The lad's eyes opened, glazed over and his lips rose in a beaming, wet smile before he slumped again and Keith had to take his weight to stop him falling to the floor.

"He's stinking drunk," the Professor said and Keith had to agree. Gerry smelled like he'd taken a bath in strong liquor without removing his clothes.

Keith turned to the other two.

"We told you before we left, no hard stuff on site, just beer."

Doug and Bill put their hands up. It was Bill who spoke for both of them.

"We brought nothing, that's the God's honest truth and we didn't see him drink anything except coffee. As I said, one minute he was fine and then..." He waved a hand in Gerry's direction; the meaning was clear.

"So, you took the bottle off him?" Keith asked.

Doug spoke up this time.

"That's what we're trying to tell you. We didn't see him drink anything except coffee. There is no bottle."

Keith managed to get Gerry back into the chair and mostly upright again before checking the coffee mug. It was empty but smelled strongly of whiskey. As he was putting it down he saw the bagged and tagged bottle of Bushmills sitting on the floor at Gerry's side.

"Don't tell me he drank this?"

The Professor came over and took the bagged bottle from Keith, checking the contents against the light.

"I don't think he's had anything out of it. As far as I can tell it's as it was when we found it. As drunk as he is, it would take a good few ounces to get him in that state."

Keith had a good look around the immediate area but saw nothing untoward. He turned back to the other two again.

"So, where's the booze? Come on, guys, give it up. Speak now, or regret it later when the truth comes out. And it will come out, I promise you that."

Neither Doug nor Bill would budge from their story and they looked sincere, confused even.

"You'll have to ask Gerry when he comes out of it," Bill said. "We can't help you. I wish we could."

As if to punctuate the statement Gerry giggled then farted loudly.

"Okay, first things first," Keith said. "Let's get this idiot to bed and let him sleep it off. We'll hear his story when he recovers. We can only hope the hangover is an epic one."

Doug and Bill helped him carry Gerry across the campsite and into their tent where they dumped the drunken youth unceremoniously into his cot and covered him with his sleeping bag. Gerry was still smiling as they backed out.

When they returned to the work tent the Professor was

examining the clay pipe they'd found in the cabin. Keith went over to his side.

"Did you take any of the seed-material from the bowl for analysis?" the Professor asked.

Keith shook his head.

"I thought it best to leave it intact for the moment."

The Professor nodded.

"I wonder, given the state of Gerry there and the lack of a liquor bottle, whether some kind of psychoactive substance might be involved?"

"Professor, he smells like a distillery. There's definitely a liquor bottle somewhere in this equation. Whiskey, if I'm not mistaken."

The Professor nodded absent-mindedly.

"I'll check the seeds under the scope anyway; you never know."

Keith poured a cup of coffee from the pot, sniffing at it to make sure the liquor wasn't in the brew itself but it was only coffee, slightly stale and not as hot as it could be but even bad coffee is good at the right time.

Now all I need is a cigarette.

He pushed the thought down again.

Work. That's what I need.

Doug and Bill stood around like a pair of loose ends.

"You two, do something useful. Get back to the cabin and collect what we left on the table. You may as well bring a couple of the sheets from the beds too but bag and tag them over there. We'll want to get samples taken from them when we get back to St. Johns and don't want them contaminated. I'll be grading you on this. Don't fuck up."

Both of them nodded and left, as if happy to get away from what was turning out to be a much worse day than any of them had anticipated.

Keith double-checked their cataloging of the morning's photographs. He didn't look too closely at the figures seated around the table at first, concentrating initially on the exterior shots. He was pleased to see they were all sharp and in focus, although in one of them, one taken of the front porch, he saw one of the small doll-like mannequins sitting on a step, legs swinging. He was absolutely sure it hadn't been there when he took the photograph. And he was doubly sure when he zoomed in on it and saw a pair of emerald-green eyes, Joanna's eyes staring back at him.

Instead of pointing it out to the Professor, he went back to the coffee machine and made up a fresh brew, almost strong enough to stand a spoon up in it. By the time he'd downed half a mug and went back to the photograph, it showed only an empty porch again.

God, I need a cigarette.

Keith took chef's duties for lunch; he needed the distraction. He put all his attention into making up baloney and cheese sandwiches, enough to feed a small army. The Professor only nibbled at his but Doug and Bill coming back laden with the finds from the old campsite made up for the Professor's lack of appetite. Keith even relented and allowed the lads a beer to wash everything down.

They ended up eating Gerry's share of the sandwiches; he was still out for the count in the tent, still farting, snoring and looking like he wouldn't surface any time soon.

After lunch, Keith had the two students catalog the finds from the cabin. The Professor hogged the microscope again, studying some of the material extracted from the clay pipe. Keith should have gone back to double checking the photographs but he was afraid what he might see there if he looked at the large figures seated round the table, afraid they might have moved, or even not be there.

He took the opportunity to do as the Professor had asked and read more of the foreman's diary. He went to the source this time, removing the bagged notebook from the plastic casing before taking it to the quiet of his and the Professor's tent. He lay down on his bunk and opened the diary carefully, slowly turning each page as the history unfolded. He found the place he had stopped the night before and continued from there.

"June 21st

"Today is a good day, one of the few we have had
since our arrival. Hope is restored, for to my immense
surprise and no small relief, we have struck silver.

"I was called to the face of shaft one early this
afternoon. By the time I got there half the crew were
crammed into the chamber for a look and the other half
were making a queue at the mouth to be given a chance
to view this, our first sign of anything but the obdurate
rock. It is a thin thread to hang by but at this stage in
our endeavors I will take whatever providence chooses
to provide.

"Malone, of course, insists on taking the credit for
the rock giving up its secret, believing his entreaties and
our libation to the Wee Folk have instigated this good
fortune. As for that and despite the excitement and con-
jecture among the men, all talk of fortune is premature,
as it is only a thin, broken, seam and will barely cover
our expenses of the operation so far.

"But it is a start and the men seem all the happier
for it. I do not know how much we will be able to dig
out with the tools we still have at hand but if Murphy
and Callaghan do not dally, they should be back within
the week with stronger metal that will better suit our
purpose.

"With the men's morale much improved and the
rock finally yielding to our efforts, the work proper, the
task we came all this way for, can finally begin.

"I am writing this at the end of a long, tiring day, for
once the vein was spotted the men had to have at it with
pick and shovel, axe and trowel, even fingers, when the
metal proved no match for the rock. I took my turn with
the rest of them and spent two hours hacking and hew-
ing until my arms ached and my head pounded with the
ringing of metal on stone but I was happy to do it. The
silver has renewed our faith, rekindled our hope.

"We only have an ounce or so to show for our effort

but it is a start and tonight the team and myself made inroads into the last of the ale to celebrate, although I forbade them, to their great chagrin, from broaching the last crate of uisque. It will be needed, I hope, for further and bigger celebrations yet to come."

Keith skipped quickly forward, speed-reading. The next week or so of pages were details of the miners' mostly frustrated attempts to get at the vein of silver with an ever-decreasing number of tools at hand. The crew turned more and more disgruntled, the beer and tobacco had run out and there was a plague of the black flies keeping everyone who wasn't working indoors, locked in the cabin most of the day. Tempers were frayed and Donnelly's worries grew daily.

Nothing happened to explain the Professor's insistence Keith read the whole diary. That obviously had yet to come.

The story picked up momentum again on the first day of the new month.

"July 1st,

"Glory be, our hope has been restored at the precise moment when it was at its lowest ebb. The last of our big picks broke this morning when Malone, it had to be Malone of course, went at the silver seam too hard. The buffoon is dashed lucky it did not rebound and crack his head, for the target was surely big enough but as it was, our best remaining tool was left in three pieces on the pit floor.

"After that, there was grumbling aplenty over the poor fare passing for lunch and I thought I might well have a full-scale mutiny on my hands. Then we heard it, the sound of a pony braying, followed by Murphy's call from outside the encampment.

"Murphy and Callaghan have returned to us, laden with new, strong, tools, four barrels of ale, a crate of fine Irish uisque, enough tobacco for an army and flour and dry biscuits to keep us provisioned through this sum-mer. If only there was something apart from the tobacco they could have brought to deal with the buggering black flies I would be happier still.

"But I will take what I can get, although I fear they were taken advantage of somewhat at the stores in Buchan and have paid too highly for the goods we have obtained. The number of promissory notes we now must make good on after the summer is done is piled far too high for my liking. I will try to keep the monetary details from the men, for their morale is high now but might not remain so for long when the reality of our situation occurs to them.

"So once again, even despite today's most welcome return, I am living on hope that this vein of silver is only the start of something much, much larger.

"I allowed the men a celebratory uisque or three and Murphy, while in his cups, chose, rather unwisely I thought, to relate to us a tale he had heard in the inn at Buchan's Junction. According to him, it pertained to the area in which we were mining and he was told it as a word of caution to be relayed to all of us, *to save our souls*, was how he rather dramatically put it.

It was a long story, as such stories often are and I will not lay it all down here, for it is all too obviously merely a tall tale to frighten away strangers, telling as it does of prospectors becoming lost to a vaguely defined devilish menace in the wilds. But the men lapped it up in the way superstitious men do when they are far from home.

"After the tale was done Douglas Franks even remarked he thought he had seen a bogle in the woods the night before when he went for a shite. It got him a laugh all round and thankfully talk quickly turned back to what was uppermost in everyone's mind, the important matter of the silver lode.

"I am not the only one here with hope it seems and the men are excited with the prospect of fortune and glory.

"Even despite my worries about the money, after today, a triumphant return to the homeland seems closer than ever before."

"July 2nd,

"We made better progress today than I could have imagined. The new tools are proving much more efficacious against the rock, the men have a renewed sense of purpose and we have brought over a ton of rubble out of the ground and into the pond this day alone. Better than that, I estimate we have to hand five or maybe even six ounces of fine silver.

"The men are sure there is more to be had and Malone, to his credit, keeps them working when I am not at the face. If he wasn't so full of his stories of the Wee Folk and so embittered at being passed over for foreman I believe we might have come to a better understanding and might even have made a bond of friendship. Perhaps it is not too late even now. If our dreams are fulfilled and we all become wealthy men he may look more kindly on my part in this matter.

"Even the blasted flies have stayed away this day, as if to give us a pause in which to be thankful for small mercies and the sun shone brightly out of a clear blue sky. There is much of beauty in this new land on days like this and I do not take enough time to stop and enjoy it. Perhaps that too will now change for the better.

"The only blot on an otherwise fine day is our first casualty, thankfully not a fatal one. In truth, I expected an injury to have happened before now, given the relative lack of experience of these men in such conditions. But this rock is tougher than Welsh coal and less prone to collapses and falls and perhaps it was this apparent stability that made one of us over rash in approaching the face.

"Murphy, fresh from his travels, was keen to be at the rock with a new pickax. He was perhaps a bit overly keen if truth is told and not quite in full control of his faculties, for he had partaken more than most of the uisque last night. He laid into the rock with rather too much gusto, throwing caution to the wind. All he succeeded in doing was bringing a slab of stone down on his left leg.

"I heard his screams from here in the cabin, even though he was down in the pit at the rock face. By the time I got there they had lifted the stone off him but his leg is gashed badly and crushed even worse. The big bones are broken in two places we can find and perhaps more.

"The poor man went as white as any man I have seen but did not cry out as we tended to him, although he did, again, partake of a prodigious amount of the liquor. We have set the leg with splints where we can and stitched up the wound as well as we are able. He cannot travel and will be abed until he heals, or succumbs.

"Either fate will not go easy with him, for there seems to an infection already spreading in the wounded leg and his veins have taken on a blackish-brown hue that does not bode well for his continued well-being. At least he is asleep, for now, the uisque having finally taken hold but I would not like to be in his shoes when he awakes on the morrow, if he awakes.

"The men have taken it sore and there are mutterings of how Murphy is reaping a fit and just reward for angering the Wee Folk with his tall tale of the night before. I have tried to nip such stories in the bud, for I know of old how quickly they can spread and fester. But I may be too late already.

"Tonight, as I was doing my inspection round before retiring, I found two small dolls cunningly woven in twig and leaf, sitting in the branches at the edge of the camp. I have met superstition in mining men before. The Welsh, after all, have whole pantheons of sprites and spirits and kobolds needing appeased in the dark and they too make dolls, from wheat sheaves and stalks, somewhat resembling these I have found.

"It appears I am not the only one with the knowledge. I think someone here is afraid enough to be making protections, totems against the wrath of the Wee Folk.

"As for myself, I never found such things in any way efficacious, nor has praying to the Almighty brought me anything but a dead wife and a lot of grief. I trust only my own judgment. I have thrown the dolls in the stove and I will make sure the men know in the morning. I will have no more of this superstitious nonsense.

"But that is only by the by. We have the tools and there is still silver in the rock waiting for us.

"Onward."

Keith closed the journal, sitting back to consider what he'd read, momentarily stunned at the mention of the sculpted dolls in this original document.

It's too similar to be merely coincidence. Maybe the Professor is right. Maybe we are not the first people in recent times to read it.

His line of thought led to far too many questions, like why the diary had been returned to the box, why it had been left in the open to be found and why there were so many of the small sculptures scattered all over the camp.

And for what purpose?

8

Gerry came up slowly out of fitful dreams of being lost in a strange, yet strangely familiar, city where no one would talk to him and everybody sang in an Irish accent.

His first coherent thought was deciding that, as he was lying down, vomiting was probably not a good idea. His head felt like it had been stuffed with wet towels, his mouth felt like a squirrel had shat in it and his guts seethed and roiled like a sea in a gale. He had no memory of anything beyond sitting in the work tent waiting for Doug and Bill to finish up with their database updates and pouring a mug of coffee from the brew pot.

What the hell was in the coffee?

He had a hangover, he knew that much at least but he had all the after effects and none of the memories of pleasure. He felt much as he had on the morning after his eighteenth birthday, after a score of tequila slammers and more than a few beers in the bars of George Street. At least then he'd had some, admittedly vague, memory of the cab trip home and the vomit trail he'd left on his mother's new hallway carpet. He had no way of knowing if he'd disgraced himself on this occasion. There was only a dark, empty hole in his mind where the time had been.

He checked under the sleeping bag. It had been draped on top of him, he was fully clothed and, although the stench of whiskey was strong it looked like he'd kept all of his bodily fluids inside rather than outside.

At least there's that to be thankful for.

The fact that it was dark outside the tent and he was lying in his cot frightened him though, for his last memory was from before noon when the sun was high in the sky.

How long was I out?

He didn't wear a watch as he usually relied on his tablet for the time and it was in his satchel, wherever that might be. The only way to find out what had happened was to get up and deal with it but it proved easier said than done. He swung his legs out of the cot, then back in again as a wave of nausea washed over him, threatening to toss him back into the black hole.

I told you it was good stuff.

The Irish voice in his head brought the memory, at least of the start of it, back, reminding him of how he'd sneaked the thick drops of liquor out of the old bottle.

Why in hell would I drink that? It could have been anything; engine oil, tar, even rat poison.

Yet he had drunk it with no hesitation whatsoever, something completely out of character and he'd done it without any worry about consequences or outcome to his health. His father would be disgusted with him. He didn't even have an excuse.

I did it because the Irishman's voice in my head told me it would be a good thing.

He didn't think it was a great defense when he had to explain it to the Professor and Keith. He didn't have a clue what he was going to tell them but he knew it was best to face it now rather than to let it fester into something even worse over time.

He gritted his teeth and finally swung his legs out of the cot, staying there for ten seconds or more to ensure his guts would cooperate before he tried to stand. When he did get upright he felt light-headed, woozy and so tired the cot looked welcoming again but his guilt was stronger than his weariness. He walked away and out of the tent to face the music.

The cold night air hit him hard and his legs went even weaker. He stumbled, not quite stable, toward the work tent from where he could hear the muffled voices of the others. As he got closer he heard snatches of the conversation. Thankfully they weren't talking about him.

"It's a local plant," the Professor said, "one of the Myrtles. And it's only partially ground seeds. Why they'd smoke them, I have no idea, unless they were growing desperate having run out of tobacco."

"It says in the diary they were running short at one point," Keith replied.

"Yes, but they got fresh supplies not long before the end. So why this?"

Gerry could only guess but it seemed they were talking about the contents of the clay pipe he'd seen Doug and Bill handle earlier. They had also spoke about the diary, stuff Gerry as yet knew nothing about. He had missed out on enough of the day already. He parted the tent flap and stepped inside, hoping they'd let him get back to work, knowing that it was unlikely.

It went as bad as he had feared.

"Ah, the Young Lochinvar," the Professor said when he saw Gerry enter but there was no smile on the older man's face. Likewise, Keith looked Gerry up and down, shook his head sadly and went back to work where he was looking down the microscope at, presumably, the contents of the pipe.

Doug and Bill smirked when Gerry looked in their direction.

"I'm sorry," Gerry began. "I don't know what happened."

"I do," Keith replied. "You got drunk as a skunk on the job, in here with all the finds. You're damned fortunate you didn't contaminate everything. If I had my way we'd kick you off the course right now. The Professor's settled for putting a note in your file, a warning if you like. Think yourself lucky."

"But I didn't..."

Keith put up a hand.

"Yes, you did. I carried you to bed. I smelled it on you. There'll be no excuses. There can be no excuses. We all saw the state you were in."

Doug and Bill were full on smiling now behind Keith. Gerry considered trying to argue his case but knew he had no evidence one way or the other. They wouldn't believe two drops of ancient whiskey would have floored him like that, never mind that he'd done it because an Irish voice persuaded him it was a good idea.

I'm not sure I believe it.

If he admitted drinking out of the old bottle, he'd be in trouble anyway for tampering with a find. He kept quiet, not able to find anything he could say to improve the situation.

"Keep out of my way," Keith said and the look of disgust was clear on his face. "I don't want to hear a word out of you for the rest of the trip. And don't touch anything. Sit in a corner and be quiet. Or fuck off out of my sight. Either way is good by me. Understood?"

Gerry looked from Keith to the Professor but there wasn't going to be any help coming from the older man. Any goodwill Gerry had built up had blown away.

The whiskey bottle he'd taken a drink from sat on the worktable near the laptop, still bagged up. There was still about an inch of dark fluid in the bottom but for now Gerry felt no compunction to have more of it and the Irish voice in his head stayed quiet.

Thank God for small mercies.

He dropped into one of the camp chairs and kept his mouth shut. All he could do was watch, try to keep track of what was going on and hope the mood of the Professor and Keith would change, even slightly, into a more favorable one.

The Professor and Keith were still discussing the seeds they'd found in the clay pipe. Gerry knew some of the bog plants had psychoactive properties, he'd read a paper earlier in the semester on the Newfoundland indigenous peoples' use of drugs as spiritual guidance but he kept quiet. He was pretty sure the Professor had read the same paper as it was in the required reading list.

And besides, they don't want to hear from me right now.

His satchel sat on the floor by the main workbench. He considered fetching it and calling home to his parents.

But what would I tell them? They don't need to know I'm in disgrace.

Besides, his father would expect it and his mother would cry. Same as it ever was.

Instead he watched what Doug and Bill entered in the laptop; they were photographing and cataloging tableware; knives, wooden spoons, pewter plates and drinking mugs. The sight of the mug woke something inside him and the Irish voice returned.

The bottle is right there, boy. You managed it before. Sneak a gulp when nobody's watching. You know you want it.

He pushed the thought down but the voice was right, he felt the thirst grow, for booze, or rather, for the particular stuff in the old bottle. It prickled inside his skull, a deep itch shouting to be scratched but he knew that to give in now would definitely mean the end of his academic career, shot down before it had barely got going.

"I won't," he muttered.

Keith looked round at him and gave him a sharp glance, so Gerry shut his mouth quickly and tried, again, to concentrate on what the other two students were doing on the laptop.

The back of his left hand itched a few minutes later. He scratched at it idly, remembering the splinters he'd sucked out of it and the stinging sap, like mild acid on his skin. The booze must have dampened the itch earlier but now he noticed it, it was the only thing he could think about. His scratching didn't help; if anything, it made matters worse and now he was convinced he had something worming around in there, immediately under his skin, something he had to get out.

He rubbed harder then scratched his fingernails, hard, over his knuckles but he only exacerbated the itch. He used all the nails of his right hand, scratching up and down from fingertips up to almost the wrist but the itch spread apace with his scrubbing.

When he looked down his left hand was red, blotchy, much worse than it had been under the influence of the sap and looking like it had taken some serious sunburn. Worse though, the large arteries under the skin were darker still, not red but brown, almost black and thick, as if someone had been tracing there with a Sharpie. When he tried to flex his fingers he met stiffening resistance, as if the blood had gone solid.

There was no pain but the stiffening was worsening and within seconds his left hand went rigid. He tried to make a fist but he couldn't move his fingers. His hand was unresponsive to any commands, curled over, almost claw like.

I'm having a stroke!

He held the hand in front of his face, studying it as if it was an alien appendage, now fused to his body. Although now fully rigid, the brown-black in the veins darkened further and the dark coloring spread over the back of the hand, the palm and fingers. Brown tendrils reached along toward his wrist and Gerry felt an itch in his forearm.

It's spreading!

He called out, a wordless cry for help. Keith threw him a disparaging glance but it quickly turned to concern. Within seconds both Keith and the Professor were at his side. He heard the Professor mutter something, a name, Murphy.

Keith tried to stretch out Gerry's hand. There was no pain, the fingers didn't give but there was a definite creak, like wood being tested for strength. Gerry screamed, not in pain, in fear.

Keith pulled back Gerry's sleeve. The veins on the inside of his forearm looked brown, turning to black. Gerry looked down and immediately got light-headed, as if another shot of booze was taking hold in his system. He couldn't seem to get enough energy to speak, let alone move and his tongue felt dry, like cold wood in his mouth. The Irishman spoke again.

Have a wee drink, lad. It'll do you good.

Even if he'd felt like answering, Gerry was now past being able to speak. Everything felt distant, as if a thick pane of glass separated him from the world outside.

"We need to get him to a doctor, fast," the Professor said. "Or this isn't going to end well for him."

It's not exactly a barrel of laughs at the moment.

There was a frenzy of activity around him, gear was being packed and tents being taken down but it was all so far away.

The Irish voice sung softly in his head.

My Bonnie lies over the ocean. My Bonnie lies over the sea.

My Bonnie lies over the ocean. Oh, bring back my Bonnie to me.

The dark called for him again and this time he went to it gladly.

9

Keith took the rutted track as fast as he thought safe and faster in places. It was an hour's drive to the hospital on the outskirts of Gander and given the rate at which the dark tracery was running through Gerry's veins it looked like it was going to be touch and go if they got there in time.

What the hell got into him? Infection? Is it contagious?

The illness had hit Gerry fast and Keith was worried to his core. Would it take the rest of them as quickly? He didn't want to die on this lonely track, hardening in his hands so driving would be impossible and left, stranded, as the infection raged and they died, alone, out here where nobody would find them for months, even years.

Every time he got a chance he looked down at his hands on the wheel, checking them for signs of the black tracery.

Is it in there already working its way through me?

Then he had to concentrate on the track again as they barreled through a series of tight curves on a narrow, vegetation-lined path.

Everything had been frantic since Gerry first let out the wail, sounding like someone in terror rather than a man in pain. The Professor said jump and thankfully they'd all complied, even the two other students who now showed none of the signs of reluctance for activity they'd had earlier.

They'd only taken twenty minutes to break camp and get the back of the truck loaded up and squared away. Even in the short time it took Gerry fell completely unresponsive and the black and brown tracery ran all the way up his left arm and clearly showed across his shoulder and onto his neck.

What happens when it reaches his brain?

It wasn't anything he wanted to be thinking about.

Keith tried to concentrate on the driving. The headlights showed a tunnel of foliage ahead of them, with whipping twigs and branches fighting against them all the way. The pickup bounced alarmingly in the ruts; he was going too fast for the conditions and the suspension was taking a real pounding. He slowed a few revs lower and the truck steadied but every fiber of him was telling Keith to hurry.

The Professor sat in the back with Gerry's head in his lap, while Bill and Doug, pale faced and wide eyed, were pushed tight together up front in the passenger seat beside Keith. Every time the truck bounced, they bounced nearly as high themselves. The lads were going to be bruised and battered by the end of the trip but neither of them complained and each cast worried glances at the back seat when the track was flat enough to give them a brief respite.

"How's he doing?" Keith shouted back at one of those rare, flatter sections.

"It's not good," the Professor said. "Drive faster."

Keith threw caution to the wind and put his foot down.

By the time they skidded off the track and onto blacktop Keith's arms and shoulders felt like he'd been engaged in heavy lifting all day and his head pounded in a tension headache. The truck had survived the battering, although it would definitely need a new paint job back in the shop in St. Johns.

Now they were on a proper road they made much better time. Keith pushed it hard. If they were to be stopped by a cop, it would all be for the best, as it would mean they'd get an escort to the Hospital. The road was quiet and mostly clear of traffic and it was less than half an hour of speed before he was able to pull in to the bay in front of the E.R. of Gander Hospital.

He and the Professor bundled Gerry out as carefully as they could manage then headed for the doors, already calling for help as they went.

"We've got a sick man here. Need some help, fast."

The system took over as soon as they got to the main reception area. Efficient young doctors arrived, took one look at Gerry and sped him away without waiting for any paperwork. After the panic at the campsite, the frantic dash along track and road and the constant roar of the truck engine in his ears, Keith was struck by the sudden silence. There was nobody else in reception now but them and the man behind the desk, who held out a sheaf of papers needing to be dealt with.

Keith left it to the Professor, who took on the role of Gerry's guardian, while the rest of them stood back. Ten minutes later they were all four sitting in the waiting area, coming down from the rush of adrenaline coursing through them. The real world slowly filled in around Keith and the buzzing of the truck's engine in his head receded, slowly, into the distance.

"They'll let us know when they know," the Professor said. Keith saw the older man had Gerry's satchel in his lap.

"Gerry lives with his parents, doesn't he?" Keith asked.

Bill nodded.

"Up in Mount Pleasant. The number should be in his phone or tablet."

The Professor dug around in the satchel and came up with a tablet. He passed it to Bill, who suddenly looked startled until the Professor managed a smile.

"Don't worry, I'll do the talking but I need you to make the call. I don't have a clue how to work one of those things."

The simple admission of incompetence broke much of the tension that had been with them since the campsite. Bill took the tablet, quickly dialed the number and passed it back to the Professor, who wandered off to one side to get some privacy. Even at a distance of some five meters Keith heard Gerry's mother's wail of horror coming through and saw the pain cross the Professor's face as he gave out the bad news.

"They're coming," was all the Professor said when he sat back down and returned Gerry's tablet to the satchel.

Keith took the chance of a period of relative calm in the chaos to head back out to the truck, move it from the front of the E.R. and park it in the public spaces farther to the left. The quiet felt too still, too dark, after the frantic activity of the last couple of hours and he was surprised to look at the dashboard clock and see it was still before midnight. It felt like half the night had passed.

From where he parked he had a clear view of the E.R. entrance. Two nurses came out, chatting animatedly and suddenly Keith thought of Joanna.

It could be me in there with the infection coursing through me. It could be me instead of Gerry. I might never see the baby… our baby.

He knew what he had to do. It was what he should have done without thinking immediately after he'd been told of the pregnancy. He got out his phone and called her number. She didn't answer, he didn't expect her to during shift hours but this time when the voicemail kicked in he left a message.

"Will you marry me? I've been an idiot, I know that but the only thing I want is you and our baby. I'm yours forever, if you'll have me."

When he closed the phone, he knew it wasn't going to be enough.

But it's a start. And it's the right start.

He felt better than he had since their row, better than he had for weeks. The realization he was going to be a father was still something he couldn't quite process but tonight's close encounter with Gerry's infection had brought home to him how fragile and temporary life could be.

It had been a lesson he needed to learn.

As he stepped out of the truck he caught a flash of green in the rear-view mirror. For a split second he was reminded of a pair of emerald eyes, staring at him but when he blinked and looked again all he saw was the black expanse of the empty parking lot.

18

Gerry dreamed.

He was at the site, stood at the mouth of the mineshafts under the overhang, looking out over a nighttime winter scene lit by a full moon. The flat patch of their campsite ground was empty and bare, although the round of stones he'd built as a hearth were still there, off center. Gerry had been left alone but somehow it didn't worry him.

The pond was still black but everything else lay under an icing sugar dusting of white. It had snowed, only a light fall but enough for him to see a clear set of footsteps leading away from the rock face down toward the campsite. Gerry was intrigued enough to follow them.

The prints were strangely short and wide and it looked like there were flecks of rotting vegetation in the marks but Gerry didn't stop and look. He was dreaming, he knew that, somewhere inside, in the same way as he knew his purpose for being here, in the dark, in the snow, was to follow.

He tracked the footprints as quickly as he was able but after a few steps he realized something else. He might be dreaming but he was also drunk. Not falling down drunk but enough to make walking in the snow a serious business. He could scarcely manage more than a stumbling waddle.

He went down the slope and across the flat camping area. There were no tire marks in the snow, so sign of where the tents had been. The others had departed before the snowfall, if they'd ever been here, in this dream.

Gerry stumbled on for a while, heading south into the wilder ground but soon the foot marks became confused with the prints of others passing this way, tiny prints he thought were birds or small rodents but on closer examination looked all too human.

The snow got deeper here and harder to push through. After only a few minutes Gerry slumped, exhausted against a tree.

Then he heard it, a high clear tenor singing an old song, one he knew by memory, one he'd also heard recently.

My Bonnie lies over the ocean,
My Bonnie lies over the sea.
My Bonnie lies over the ocean.
Oh bring back my Bonnie to me.

He followed the sound and entered a campsite. There were three timber huts here, two small, one much larger, all recently built by the look of them but all silent and empty.

The song stopped as soon as Gerry stepped into the circle of cleared ground. A figure, a bent, hunched over, man wearing a heavy overcoat covering him from chin to toes, stood across the clearing under an overhanging mountain ash. Gerry called out to him.

"Hello?"

He got no reply. He heard a noise, crackling and a rustling but there was no sign he had been heard. He moved closer, noticing the figure must have been the one he had been following, as there was only a single clear set of prints again in the snow here and like the prints, the man in front of him was stocky. He had a mass of bushy hair that hung down his back. In the gloom and dim light under the trees it looked almost green.

As Gerry got within five meters he spoke again.

"Hello?"

There was still no reply. He went over and touched the man's shoulder, then stood back as the figure turned around. The man didn't just look green; he was green, his skin more like the bark of a tree than flesh, a long beard bristling and firm and bright, like new pine needles. Two deep emerald green eyes were sunk deep into dark, almost black hollows but they sparkled with life.

The worst thing was the mouth; Gerry couldn't take his eyes off it. The lips were thin, almost non-existent, pulled back over red, feverish gums in which three brown teeth, looking almost wooden sat, spaced at intervals in the rotting tissue. The tongue sliding in and out when he looked up at Gerry was also brown and solid. It gleamed like a lump of varnished and polished wood.

For his left hand, the man only had a foot-long crooked stick of dark wood. He pointed at a leaf in his right palm, a brown leaf from last year's fall. As Gerry watched it went green, from the edges first, a yellowing then a darkening spreading inward along the veins, crackling and rustling as the leaf unfurled and stretched before falling to the ground.

Gerry looked down at white roots running in a frenzy at his feet, seething and crawling over and around each other like a slithering nest of snakes. All around the clearing new growth rose up from the circle of gravelly ground.

The stick pointed again, this time at a Myrtle bush. Buds grew, leaves opened and fresh berries reddened and ripened in the space of a single breath. Gerry didn't know why but he found he was crying.

When he looked up again the squat figure had wandered off, over into the center of the campsite next to the largest of the timber huts. Gerry followed. As he got closer he saw the figure had bent over something on the ground. He heard cooing noises coming from the festering hole which passed as a mouth. A small bird fluttered feebly on the ground. The man pointed the stick at it.

"No" Gerry shouted.

The green man looked round at him and pointed at Gerry's chest. He felt emotion well up inside him and unbidden the song came. He stood there in the middle of the campsite and sang until his heart swelled.

Yeah bring back, oh bring back,
Oh bring back my Bonnie to me to me.

The green man waved the stick in time, as if conducting the song and smiled a huge grin showing his few remaining teeth as Gerry finished. Then he did something even more remarkable than anything Gerry had already seen. He pointed the stick at his chest then at Gerry and repeated the action. Every time he did so Gerry felt emotion rise and fall inside him, like the swell of the ocean and he heard the song, clear as day, ringing in his head.

The green man pointed at the green shoots on the ground then at Gerry, backward and forward and he raised a bushy eyebrow in a question. Gerry was not exactly sure what was being asked of him but he knew one thing and knew it well; he wanted to feel the swelling, the life... he wanted it more than anything else in the world.

He'd thought the call of the old liquor bottle had been strong but this was stronger. It spoke to him, deep in his soul, in his bones, in every cell of his being.

I want this.

The green man pointed the stick again at Gerry's chest.

Gerry nodded.

Several things happened at once. The green man passed Gerry the stick. At the same moment Gerry looked to the ground to see both the man's legs were now sunk deep into the ground while white roots slithered across his whole lower torso. The stick writhed in Gerry's hand and he felt a slight pain as it took root, nestling in his palm as if it had been grown there. Green veins spread up his arm and Gerry smiled as the thin needles of a new green beard sprouted on his chin.

The green man smiled in return, even as the roots tugged violently at him and his body fell apart into a moist brown loam quickly turning green.

The song rose up in Gerry and could not be contained. He walked through the campsite singing and waving the stick in time:

Bring back, oh bring back,
Oh bring back my Bonnie to me to me.
Oh bring back, oh bring back,
Oh bring back my Bonnie to me.

Spring followed behind him.

PART 2: INTO THE BLACK

1

The night in the waiting room felt never ending. Keith spent most of it waiting for his phone to ring, even though he knew Joanna rarely checked her messages before coming off shift. He kept going over in his mind what he'd said in the voice mail, wondering if he'd been too strong, wondering whether she'd forgive him… anything to keep his mind off what might be happening to poor Gerry elsewhere in the hospital.

The other three kept quiet for the most part. Doug had lost his usual swagger and looked more like the schoolboy he must have been only a few years previously. Bill wept quietly for a time, leaving him with red, rheumy eyes, rimmed with dark shadows brought on by the lack of sleep. The Professor sat, head down and Keith thought he might be sleeping but he wasn't snoring and like the rest of them, he looked up expectantly, at every door opening, every sound of footsteps in the corridor.

They drank insipid coffee from an elderly wheezing machine, ate candy bars and every twenty minutes or so made small talk, trying to avoid mention of Gerry. For what felt like endless hours there was no news of any kind.

Then everything happened at once.

Gerry's parents turned up at four a.m. They looked tired and flushed but Keith knew them immediately; the man had a strong resemblance to the boy. The four of them stood and went to meet the arriving couple in the reception area.

"What's he gone and done this time," the father asked. If there was any worry or concern there, he hid it well but the mother was making up for both of them. She too had been weeping, her mascara running in black trails on her cheeks, reminding Keith far too much of the tracery on Gerry's arms.

Much to Keith's relief the Professor took charge again.

"He took ill out at the campsite," he said.

"Was it his asthma?" Gerry's mother said. "He suffered terribly as a child and..."

The father interrupted.

"I don't think we'd have been called out here in the middle of the night for an asthma attack." He turned to the Professor "How bad is it?"

The Professor shook his head.

"It's not for me to say. I'm no doctor."

Gerry's mother broke in again and there were fresh tears at the corners of her eyes, more mascara running.

"But it's bad, isn't it?"

The Professor was saved from answering. At almost the same moment, one of the young doctors came through from the wards. He looked at the Professor, then at the parents and instinctively made the right choice, taking the parents off to one side and speaking softly.

They talked in urgent whispers and Keith only heard snatches, out of context words like infection, unresponsive, stable, enough to know it wasn't great news but better than he'd feared.

The Professor stepped over to join the parents once the doctor was finished. He also spoke in whispers and Keith didn't pick up anything until the last sentence.

"This is his," the Professor said, handing over the satchel before the doctor whisked the man and woman away and the four of them were once again left in the quiet, suddenly empty again, waiting room.

"Is it bad?" Bill asked as soon as the Professor walked back toward them.

"It's not good, that's for sure. Gerry has some kind of infection that appears to have started in the wounds on his hands. They're working on it and have stabilized him but Gerry hasn't woken up yet. They say he's unresponsive, which I'm guessing means coma. They've got him on a variety of meds and a dialysis machine. They hope to know more later in the morning."

Bill looked like he might cry again and Doug looked ready to join him. Keith meanwhile focused on one word... wounds.

"Is anyone else scratched or have a splinter?" the Professor asked. Keith realized it was something they should all have considered sooner but caution had been lost in the rush to get Gerry to the E.R. and although he'd checked his hands many times in the interim, he hadn't been looking for punctures in particular.

They all, rather self-consciously, checked their hands and forearms but although they had minor scratches and abrasions from pushing through rough foliage, none of them had deep splinter holes like those Gerry had sported and none of them showed any sign of blackening in the veins.

"It looks like we're all okay," the Professor said. "I wish we could say the same for young Gerry."

"There's brain activity though?" Keith asked but the Professor only shrugged.

"The doctor didn't say and I didn't think to ask. You now know as much as I do and as much as his parents do, for what that's worth."

Keith checked his watch. It was still only a quarter after four. The night was passing deliberately slowly.

"So, what now? Back to the site?" he asked. "We could do some rooting around once it's light?"

The Professor shook his head.

"We'd only have to leave again to go home in the afternoon and I think we collected most of what we needed for a first visit. Besides, until we know exactly what Gerry's got, it might not be safe to return. Are you up to driving us home?"

"And leave Gerry alone?" Bill said.

"His parents are here now. What with them and the doctors, he's in good hands. We'd only be in the way. We did our bit, as much as we could. We got him here in time. Now I think we should head home."

The Professor looked at Keith and Keith nodded in reply to the question he saw in the man's eyes. He was tired but he was also wired. Given a choice between trying to catch a few hours of cramped sleep in the truck or driving four hours down the road to a waiting bed, he'd take the drive.

There was only one other car in the parking bay as they left the E.R., probably the one belonging to Gerry's parents. Keith checked the rear mirror anyway, looking for any flash of green, any staring, emerald eyes but there was only the flat black of the empty parking bay back there as he pulled out and drove back onto the highway heading east.

It was a cold, clear night and for the most part they had the road to themselves after leaving Gander behind. The stresses of the past hours took their toll of the other three almost immediately, as if the noise of the pickup's engine was a lullaby and the roll of tires on the road a rocker. They'd barely gone ten kilometers before the two lads in the back fell asleep.

That's probably for the best. At least it'll stop young Bill fretting.

The Professor tried to keep alert longer, perhaps hoping to help keep Keith awake on the drive but the older man's thought processes were jumbled and confused. He spoke of infection, of Irish legends and of the diary but to Keith's mind it wasn't making much sense.

"Gerry's infection has something to do with the diary? The nonsense with the wooden dolls and the ceremony in the mineshaft, you think it's connected? How is that possible?"

"How much of it did you read?" the Professor asked.

"Still only half; I got up till the point where Murphy has his accident."

The Professor nodded and had trouble raising his head again; the older man looked shattered and ready to wilt.

"When we get back you need to finish it. Then we'll talk."

"What about?" Keith asked but the Professor had succumbed to the same lullaby as the two in the back. His head fell forward and he was gone and lost in sleep.

Keith didn't feel much tiredness. He enjoyed driving the big truck on the quiet, straight road and pushed her up to a few km over the speed limit. If he was on his own he'd be going even faster and have the classic rock station on, loud, for company but with the other three asleep he decided to let them rest.

Now he had time to think, he made connections between what the Professor had been talking about, Gerry's sudden illness and the infection to Murphy's leg in the journal. There also was a correlation between Gerry's apparent drunkenness and the libations to the Wee Folk the miners had made and to the wood sculptures and how they might relate to the dolls the foreman had mentioned in his diary. Like the Professor's talk before going to sleep, it was all of a jumble and he couldn't grasp onto anything to let him draw a firm conclusion.

And I'm not going to get anywhere with it at this time of the morning.

He drove with his reflexes and muscle memory; there was next to no traffic to negotiate, just him, the truck and the road unfolding below them. It felt like he was alone in the world and not for the first time he wondered what it would be like to keep going, driving into the dawn and not stopping, into the great beyond to see where the road took him.

This particular road wasn't going anywhere he didn't know though; home was at the eastern end of the Trans-Canada Highway in St. Johns where the road stopped at the sea. All of Canada was along this same road but for the moment at least it was all behind him, receding in the rear-view mirror. With every passing minute his options were narrowing not expanding.

It got him thinking of Joanna again, wondering whether she'd got his earlier message, wondering whether he'd spoken too rashly due to the adrenaline rush of the flight to the hospital, wondering if she was even going to speak to him.

They didn't need gas but his thoughts were tumbling too fast, interfering between him and even the small amount of concentration he needed for the drive. He pulled in to the Clarenville Irving station when he saw the lights ahead.

The others didn't wake up, even after he parked up at the pumps. He put thirty bucks' worth of gas in the tank and went inside to pay.

"Thirty for gas," the youth behind the till said. "Is that all?"

"Yeah. And a pack of Marlboro Red, please."

The words were out without thinking about them, the old habit resurfacing involuntarily. He knew it was the drive bringing it on; he always liked having a smoke with the window rolled down on long drives. Now he'd said the words and the smokes were on the counter in front of him, he didn't want to take them back.

"I'd better take one of these too."

He took a cheap plastic lighter from the display at the counter, thanked the kid, paid and left, already peeling the wrapping from the pack and looking forward to the first drag.

The Professor looked over blearily as Keith got back into the driving seat.

"Are we there yet?" he said with a thin smile.

"Go back to sleep, there's still a good few hours of road below us."

The Professor was asleep again even as Keith pulled back out onto the highway and he'd started snoring lightly, the same goose honk as before but at least this time it was mostly obscured by engine noise.

Keith rolled down the window on his side, lit up the first of what would be several smokes and floored the pedal. He didn't notice it but he sang softly as he drove toward the oncoming dawn.

My Bonnie lies over the ocean,
My Bonnie lies over the sea.
My Bonnie lies over the ocean.
Oh bring back my Bonnie to me.

2

Gerry didn't know whether he was asleep or awake. He remembered being in the tent, in disgrace, then there had been dreams, green dreams, so vivid they had the heft and solidity of reality. He remembered the green man, felt the stick take root in his palm and the swelling of emotion as the song had carried him away into the green. Now he had seemingly woken up but somehow this didn't feel as real and solid as his time in the snowy clearing.

He was lying on his back, staring at a too-bright light in a sterile white ceiling. He wasn't alone. He heard his mom speaking but he couldn't turn his head in the direction of her voice and although his eyes felt dry and gritty he was unable to even blink.

Am I paralyzed?

"What's wrong with him?" his mom said.

A voice Gerry didn't recognize replied.

"He has a severe infection and it's nothing with which we're familiar, nothing anybody seems to know anything about. Whatever it is, it's rare and it's nasty. We've stabilized it, for now at least. We're trying a soup of antibiotics and we're flushing him out on the dialysis machine you see."

Dialysis? What the fuck is going on here?

"What about the black stuff in his veins?" Gerry's dad said. There was a tremor in the voice Gerry didn't associate with his father. It was rare for him to show much of any concern for Gerry's well-being. That, more even than the fact he was paralyzed, told Gerry it was serious. "Can't you get it out of him?"

"That's what I mean about the infection," the doctor replied. "It's some kind of blood clotting agent but as I say, I've never seen anything like it. Under the scope it almost looks like his blood cells have developed a cellulose coating."

It wouldn't mean anything to Gerry's mom and dad but Gerry had taken a biology semester and it didn't sound good to him.

What do you mean cellulose? I'm not a fucking plant. And what's this shit about dialysis?

He thought he was shouting but no sound came out and the others in the room kept talking, even as Gerry shouted louder.

Hey. I'm right here.

Except he knew he wasn't here. It still felt dream-like to him, making him a spectator into his own life. He floated adrift from any reality, light-headed, remnants of the black booze still surging in his system. The voices of the others came slightly muffled, as if filtered through a set of cheap headphones.

Mom?

"Look," she said, "He's awake."

"No," the doctor said. "His eyes are open but he's non-responsive."

A huge face loomed over him, looking down from straight above.

"Gerry? It's mom. I'm right here, darling. Can you hear me?"

Hi, mom. I'm okay.

"Why won't he answer?" she replied. A hot tear fell onto Gerry's cheek. He felt it run across his skin and end up at his right earlobe.

That's something at least.

He couldn't move to brush it away and although he sobbed, a gut reaction to seeing his mom's distress, his own tears wouldn't come in reply.

Well, this is fucking marvelous.

"Can we at least sit him up?" Mom said, still looming over him and staring deep into his eyes, almost as if she was reading his mind. "If he is able to see us, or hear us, it must be driving him mad staring at the ceiling."

"He's non-responsive," the doctor replied. "I don't..."

"He's not your son," Mom replied angrily. Gerry had never heard her so fierce, never seen her face contorting in sudden anger so swiftly. It did the job though, for the doctor relented.

A minute later Gerry's viewpoint changed as the bed cranked up at his back, the doctor leaned him forward to rearrange his pillows and he was finally able to look across the room. His view was limited to what was right in front of him; he still couldn't turn his head. It was a big improvement.

He was definitely in hospital but where he had no idea. He didn't have much experience of hospitals and this looked like the kind of generic room he saw in TV shows, being bland, pale and somehow depressing. Both his parents looked tired and frazzled and even the doctor looked like he hadn't got much sleep.

How long have I been out of it?

He looked down the length of his body; a thin blanket covered most of it but his arms were bare. His left arm had several needles in it, attached to either a drip bag or to tubes sucking at him, greedily. He guessed the sucking was the dialysis machine's doing.

The tubes and needles were scary enough but they were nowhere as scary as what had happened to his right arm. Dark veins ran through the too-pale flesh, black down at the finger and hand, all the way to his elbow, turning to lighter brown up to his shoulder, the limit of where he could see. He recalled the doctor's description of his cells.

Cellulose? How the fuck did that get into me? And what's it doing there?

Gerry remembered the woody figures around the table in the old cabin. In remembering, he also remembered the dream, of the decaying green man who handed him a stick. He was coming to a theory about how the large dolls had gotten there and he didn't like the thought.

Wood for the wooden. Is this how it starts? Will mom look round and see a mannequin of twig and leaf, all that's left when the rest is eaten away?

He felt panic rise up. The sound of blood pumping joined

the slosh and thud from the dialysis machine as it adjusted
to the change in his blood pressure. Again, his mom read his
mind. She bent over the bed to look Gerry in the eye.

"That doesn't sound normal. What's happening?"

The doctor came over and moved Gerry's mom gently aside
so he too could look into his eyes.

What's up, Doc?

"This might be good news. He might be coming out of it,"
the doctor said and went to the door, shouting for a nurse.

Mom came over to the bedside and took Gerry's hand, his
right hand, the one with the black tracery running over it.

No! Don't do that, mom!

The beat of the drum got stronger and the slosh and thud
of the machines he was hooked up to came in on the back-beat,
like a well drilled rhythm section.

Mom stroked the back of his hand. The black veins writhed
and squirmed, spreading roots in a speeded up time-lapse
movie. Mom kept stroking. The roots writhed faster.

No, mom, get away.

She only held his hand tighter. It was as if she could not see
the spread and squirm of the blackness as it traced itself over
the back of his hand and then up, eagerly, burrowing into her
fingertips, knuckles, across the back of her hand. On her skin it
didn't look quite so black.

It looked green, fresh, growing.

No!

Gerry shouted. The drum beat went up another notch,
driving all rational thought away with it and Gerry drifted
away, not into the black but into the green, where a little Irish
voice sang him down into oblivion again with the now familiar
lullaby.

Oh, bring back my bonnie to me, to me.

3

Keith arrived in St. John's in time to finally catch some traffic, a tailback on the ring road delaying them for the first time on the trip but they were still back in the parking bay at Memorial before nine.

He had to wake the other three; even cutting off the engine didn't rouse them. The Professor was particularly bleary and stumbled stiffly out of the truck, taking a few steps before having to stop and stretch.

"Remind me not to do that again," the older man said. "I can imagine medieval tortures with better outcomes."

Keith let the other three do most of the unpacking; he considered it his reward for letting them sleep. When it came to carting everything up to the lab and office, he took pity on the Professor, whose back was obviously suffering and schlepped up and down several flights of stairs with heavy gear before they had everything out of the truck.

By the time they had the gear and the finds stowed away and secured to the Professor's satisfaction all four of them were about ready to drop.

"Do you need us for anything?" Doug asked.

If nothing else we've improved his work ethic.

The Professor shook his head.

"Get yourselves home and get some rest. This lot can wait until tomorrow. And thanks, lads."

"What for?" Bill asked.

"For not panicking in the face of a rough time, for one. And not whining. We might make field archaeologists out of you yet."

The two students left in a better mood than they'd been just seconds before. Keith grabbed his backpack, intending to follow them out.

"Hang on, Keith," the Professor said. "I want to phone the hospital and check on Gerry."

Keith waited, hearing only one side of the conversation. It appeared there was no change in Gerry, good news in one respect, bad news in another.

It was ten a.m. by the time Keith left the building and he stood in the doorway trying to decide where to go. A bar sounded awfully tempting, for Joanna would be in bed, sleeping off her night shift and he would have the excuse he didn't want to wake her. Besides, she wasn't expecting him back until later in the evening, before she had to go out to work again.

The bar it is then. And it'll be rum, plenty of rum.

He walked over to the bus stop but when the shuttle bus heading downtown arrived, he was still smoking a cigarette, so he didn't get on it.

The small, missed opportunity changed the whole course of his day, for the thought of waiting another half an hour for the next bus immediately changed his mind again. He walked away, heading across the main road, past the Holiday Inn and through the streets to his apartment block.

Our apartment block.

He still had trouble dealing with the fact they had moved in together, even though four months had already passed. Having another person in the flat still made it feel cramped sometimes and he missed sitting in his underpants in front of the TV with beer and pizza. He walked faster and was almost running as he climbed the stairs. He wanted to see her. After Gerry's close call he needed to see her, to remind him of life, rather than death.

At first, he wasn't sure she was home. The apartment felt too quiet. He kept the noise down on entering in any case, as he knew how cranky Joanna got if woken up prematurely on a shift day. Joanna snored lightly, nowhere near the extent of the

Professor's honking but usually loud enough for it to be heard through the bedroom door. There was no sound and the place didn't feel right; it felt empty, a void waiting to be filled.

She hasn't come home. I didn't piss her off that badly did I?

When he went through to the bedroom, opened the door carefully to avoid creaks and peered in he saw her sleeping form under the bedcovers. From here he definitely heard her breathing.

Something inside him he hadn't realized was tight relaxed and he backed away from the doorway, closing it gently on the way out. He knew better than to get in there with her. He headed for a shower and then brushed his teeth. As he did so he tasted stale cigarette smoke in his mouth.

I shouldn't have been smoking. Why in hell did I do that?

After freshening up, he felt wired all over again and sleep was farther away than ever. The bedroom door was still closed so either Joanna hadn't yet noticed he was home or she was still ignoring him. Either way she would be asleep for a while yet and he needed to be doing something, anything, to avoid the call of the downtown bars and the equally loud call of the pack of smokes in his jacket pocket.

He made a mug of coffee, got the laptop out of his pack and began uploading their weekend's work to the main faculty server. It was slow going, for although the wi-fi connection was pretty good, the photographic files were all high-definition and each took its own sweet time in loading upstream.

Keith had plenty of time to think but it wasn't doing him much good. If he wasn't thinking about Joanna, he worried about Gerry and the black tendrils that had crawled through him. They were still no closer to knowing what brought on the sudden infection. He remembered the Professor's words from the drive.

When we get back you need to finish it. Then we'll talk.

While the file uploads did their thing, Keith paged through the diary pages to find the spot where he'd left off.

The tale got going again the next day after Murphy's accident in the mineshaft.

"July 3rd

"I fear we have a calamity on our hands, one that might yet mean the abandonment of this camp, our dreams and all our hopes for a better life. Yesterday's accident in the shaft has proved to be far more severe than we first anticipated.

"Poor Murphy is lost somewhere deep in his dreams and cannot be roused, even by the taste of the uisque and has been that way for some number of hours now. Perhaps it is for the best, for the infection, if that what has hold of him, has taken root somewhere deep inside, denying all of our attempts to discern its source.

"His blood runs in spider-web tracery of black ink for the whole length of his damaged leg. It spreads at a frightening pace and encroaches fast on his hip and groin. At this rate, it will be above his waist in a matter of hours and if it reaches his heart I fear the worst.

"I have taken Murphy away from the others to tend to him here in our storeroom and forbidden all but myself and Jack Kelly from looking at the stricken man. Jack has some field medical knowledge from his Army days but he says he has seen nothing like this dark malignancy, even in the tropical jungles where there are more things to kill you than please you. But I am determined to keep this latest calumny quiet, for now at least. There are enough rumors abroad of spooks, bogles and haunts without me adding a disease, or even plague, to the growing hysteria.

"It was those blasted dolls that started this latest outflow of superstitious nonsense. They were seen and taken note of before I spotted them and threw them in the fire. And this morning when we woke there were more of them, in the crooks of trees, sitting by the side of the pond, even down by the dark water at the bottom of shaft two. A score or more of them, it must have taken quite some time in their making. If I find out who is behind it I shall tan their hide and frog-march them out of here forthwith.

"Of course, the men would have it that it is the Wee Folk, up to their old mischief in the new country. I have made it plain I have no time for such unchristian sentiment and have reminded the men that we are miners, not children fearful of the dark. Still, I had a hard task in persuading anyone to work the seam today and it was only the reminder of the silver so close at hand that finally got the crew moving.

"We had better make some larger find soon for these meager pickings will not hold for long against the men's innate superstition."

"July 4th

"Matters have by no means improved, indeed they get darker by the hour.

"The rock is taking its dashed time in yielding up its treasure and making us work like Trojans for even a glimmer of the silver. It is back breaking work, leaving us all bone tired and muscle weary, a condition only worsening with each passing day. The weather has not helped, for although it is still high summer there is a clammy dampness to the air that clings like cold sweat and refuses to ever get warm.

"Despite my orders to the contrary there have been several more of those blasted creations of twig and branch found in the trees circling our camp here. And yet none of the men will admit to their making and I see in their eyes; the matter is more than passing strange to them now; it has them fearful and frightened. Even Malone has refrained from his usual bluster and bravado and the mood in the camp is somber.

"It will be more somber still if what I fear for the morrow comes to pass.

"Murphy is dying, at least, I hope he is, for a man should not be asked to live in such straits as those to which he has been reduced.

"The black tracery covers all of his lower body from chest to toes, as if a crazed child has painted his skin with a network of black threads and veins, all of which pulse and throb in time with the ever more rapid beat of his straining heart. Kelly tells me if it reaches his brain, then it will most certainly be over. I can only thank providence Murphy has not awakened these past twenty-four hours and if he does pass, as now looks inevitable, it is likely to be as peaceful as it can be under the circumstances.

"This afternoon while the rest of the men were working the seam, Kelly suggested blood-letting might ease some of the pressure on Murphy's heart. He looked to me for an agreement I was glad to give, for I have discovered watching a man die slow is worse by far than seeing one go fast.

"I was of a mind to leave Jack to the task alone, for I am not overly fond of the sight of either a surgeon's knife or the letting of blood but he bade me stay, pleading he might need help should Murphy awaken suddenly. So, I stayed, averting my eyes as the cut was made in the artery in the thigh of Murphy's good leg. It was only Jack's startled exclamation that made me look around.

"I need not have been worried about feeling queasy, for there was no blood, no trace of red to be seen. The new wound gaped, a one-inch scar but inside the cut the tissue looked dry and brown. Kelly bade me touch the exposed flesh, which I did gingerly, only to feel a cold, almost icy, smoothness. It looked and felt like the bark of a branch of a cold ash tree, one but recently touched by the ice of winter."

Keith came awake with a start, woken by movement in the bedroom and was surprised, both to find he had been asleep with his head in his arms, sitting at the kitchen table and also to see it was nearly two p.m. The drive had taken more out of him than he thought and he'd zoned out but despite the hours of slumber, he didn't feel rested.

He was vaguely aware he'd been dreaming, green dreams of writhing vegetation, laughing and singing and he tasted whiskey on his tongue, although hard liquor hadn't passed his lips in days.

There was another noise in the bedroom. Joanna was moving

around and he heard the internal door to the bathroom open and the taps run.

His laptop showed the upload was done. He checked his email. There were no messages from the Professor about Gerry, which he chose to take as good news. He closed the machine down then went through to the small kitchen to get some food going, while the old plumbing knocked and wheezed under the strain of Joanna's shower.

The small acts of domestication managed to divert him, for a while at least, from considering the parallels between poor Murphy's ordeal and young Gerry, who apparently had caught a similar infection but hopefully not the same consequences.

He could scarcely imagine the foreman's anguish, having to sit and watch as those damned black tendrils ate their way through a man, out in the wilds with no hope of any medical attention, knowing only he could do nothing but let it take its course to the inevitable conclusion.

Then Joanna came out of the bedroom and all thoughts of mines and miners, infection and poor Gerry back in Gander were forgotten when she smiled at him.

Everything's going to be okay.

"Did you mean it?" she said as she stepped into a hug. She smelled of soap and hair conditioner. It took him a second to realize she meant the voicemail message he'd left for her.

"I meant every word," he replied and realized as he said it that it was true. The short trip to the wilds had changed him, more than he would have thought possible forty-eight hours previously.

"Then in that case, the answer's yes," she said.

She leaned into a kiss. Their lips touched but only briefly, before she pulled back.

"You've been smoking."

The lie came far too easily to him.

Maybe I haven't changed much after all.

"Nope. It was one of the students in the back of the truck. I had the window down but you know what it's like. It gets everywhere."

"Why did you let him smoke?"

"We were under a bit of stress."

She must have seen something in his eyes.

"Did anything go wrong? Are you okay?"

"I'm fine. One of the lads, Gerry, fell ill and we had a rush to get him to Gander."

There was nothing for it but to tell her the whole story; it acted as a pretty good foundation for his lie after all. Once he'd got the story as far as Gerry's arrival in the E.R. Joanna asked about the lad's condition but Keith could only give her what he knew.

He thought there might be even more questions but she didn't know Gerry, and her own happiness at his telephone message proposal was the overriding thing in her mind. She even believed him about the smoking but there was no more kissing.

There was, however a lot of excited chat about all the plans to be made and all of the things to be done. There was a never-ending list of duties they would both need to fulfill to organize a wedding before she got too far gone in the pregnancy itself.

Most of it washed over him; it was too much to take in all at once.

All Keith could think about was black growth, tracing through veins and the fact that a new chapter of his life had begun with a lie.

4

Gerry came out of the green slowly.

This time he was alone, sitting upright, able to see the whole room but still completely immobile, no matter how much concentration he put into moving his arms or legs. He was uncomfortably aware of the slosh and thrum of the machinery on his left-hand side. He knew it was trying to flush out the bad but it didn't feel natural; it felt like being continuously drained, emptied and hollowed out, as if being prepared for something else to fill him. He remembered the black veins, running away from him and across his mom's hand.

It was another dream. A bad dream caused by the drugs they've given me.

No matter how hard he tried he wasn't able to believe it. The longer he lay there alone the more the idea worked at him, the worry burying itself deep in his mind, refusing to be shifted. He needed to tell somebody.

Hello! Mom?

The shout was loud in his head but he knew his mouth hadn't opened. He had never felt so helpless.

Am I any better? Will I be like this forever?

He looked at his right arm, looking for signs of progress. What he saw gave him his first faint hope. The tracery was fainter than before, less distinct. But it was still there, still growing inside him. He felt it in the hollow places, an interior itch he'd never be able to scratch. He heard it too, alongside the throb of the dialysis machine, a whispering rustle like dry leaves in the wind, echoing inside him.

Alongside that, he still had the single image in his mind

refusing to go away, of his mom returning to find only what was left of him after the feeding, a wooden sculpture, freshly green, yellowing at the edges.

The rustling inside him got louder as if emboldened by the thought. His right arm tingled all the way up to the shoulder, like he'd woken from having slept on it for hours. His fingers twitched, drumming stiffly, involuntarily, on the bedcover.

Help!

No one came.

It was an age before anyone arrived. All Gerry could do was endure the maddening itch in his arm, listen to the sound of foliage rustling in his head and watch the patterns of light and shade dancing on the walls as the sun moved around outside. It wasn't his idea of entertainment.

At least the damned Irishman has stopped singing.

He wondered if he was the only one afflicted like this. Had the others caught this infection, whatever it was? Were they in other beds in other rooms, maybe even right next door? Or were they still back at the site, still in danger? He had no way of finding out and no way of asking.

He wasn't hungry, although as far as he was aware it was a full day at least since he'd last eaten. He was thirsty, though, dried out to the point of being parched. Out of nowhere, from not having given it a thought, all he could think about was the dark, viscous liquor he'd tasted from the old bottle, the moment when his problems all started.

There was no explanation he could think of as to why he'd taken the drink in the first place. He'd wanted it and he'd had it, with no conscious thought in the way between desire and action. Now he wanted more. He wanted to drown in it, to let it wash him away into oblivion, darkness, anywhere but this... locked in a nightmare in the hospital bed.

When a nurse finally came in to check on him he almost cried out in relief.

Thank God. I thought you'd all forgotten about me.

She bent over and looked straight into his eyes. He saw the

oval-shaped mole at the side of her mouth, saw the concern in her dark brown eyes but he could do nothing to get her attention as she turned to check on the dialysis machine.

My eyes are fine. Check my arm. Please. Check my arm. But don't touch me. Please, don't touch me.

His attempts got more desperate as she came back to his side and lifted his right arm to check his pulse.

No! Please don't. It's not safe.

As it had been with his mother, so it was again. The dark tracery ran quickly across her skin, fading even as it went up her fingers and over the back of her hand. She moved around the bed and kept checking his feeds even as the tracery grew over the back of her hand, heading for her wrist. It was obvious she could not see what he saw.

Gerry looked into her eyes, wondering if he might see the black veins take root in there too but there was only the same, soft, concerned look there as the nurse turned away. If she'd felt anything of the infection entering her she didn't show it.

Now the maddening, high-pitched Irish voice was back in Gerry's head again and it definitely sounded happy.

Bring back, bring back, oh bring back my bonnie to me, to me.

The nurse never turned around and never looked back. Once again Gerry was left alone but it was only for a matter of seconds. Gerry's mom and dad came back into the room. His dad didn't want to even look at the bed. He went straight over to stand by the window, staring, unseeing, into the far distance.

His mom came and sat in the bedside chair. Gerry had a good long look at her but there was no sign of the tracery, no evidence she was sick.

Have I been hallucinating again? Is this all part of the same fever dream?

Another thought struck him.

Am I going insane? Or am I already there?

Somehow, insanity would be preferable to the idea he might be some kind of Typhoid Mary, spreading the tracery wherever he touched, or rather, whoever touched him, for he had no choice in the matter.

Is this permanent?

Fear grew big inside him, blotting everything out for a while. His mom's gaze went to the machines he was hooked up to.

"His heart rate's way up again," she said, almost shouting. "Why aren't they doing anything to help him?"

"Maybe there's nothing they can do," his father said and tears ran down the man's cheeks. The single small show of weakness convinced Gerry he was in real trouble, possibly fatal trouble.

The dialysis machine thudded faster and the draining sensation felt much worse. The rustling was back in force and the tingling, pricking sensation became more than an itch; there was definitely something inside him.

And it's growing fast.

By now his mom had run to the door, shouting for help. The doctor arrived soon afterwards. This time he didn't say anything about "good signs"; he looked concerned.

Do something! Just don't touch me.

"We need to get his heartbeat down," the doctor said. "We'll give him a sedative, put him under completely for a time. It might give his body a chance to fight for him."

Get this fucking thing out of me. It's eating me alive.

Gerry shouted and screamed but only inside the cell in his mind. After they hooked him up with another drip, it felt warm and soft and sent a cozy, fluffy cotton dreaminess coursing through him.

He let go and drifted, falling away, down into the green.

5

Keith's promise not to have another cigarette lasted only as long as Joanna was still with him through the afternoon. As soon as she left for her night shift… and he did get a kiss this time, the urge grew in him fast. The lack of sleep from the night before finally caught up to him and he was ready to lie down but the call of the Marlboro was stronger. It wasn't strong enough to risk having a smoke in the flat though, her nose was too good for him to get away with that.

Only ten minutes after Joanna had gone, he left the apartment, went down to the communal courtyard in the quadrangle made by the four blocks and sat on the bench under a tall, straggly, birch, eagerly sucking in smoke.

The habit had come back without any conscious thought but he couldn't pretend he didn't enjoy it. He was fully aware that lying to Joanna was probably the worst thing he could do for his relationship but the habit was stronger than the guilt, for now.

I'll only have the one, to take the edge off.

He smoked two, right down to the butt, one right after the other before finally heading back inside. If the night hadn't suddenly gone chilly as a breeze whistled though the quadrangle he might have lit up another; the habit had come back strong.

When he put the pack away in his inside pocket he saw he only had four left.

I'll finish them tomorrow, then there'll be no more. I owe it to her. Hell. I owe it to myself.

He'd been down this route before, when he'd first met Joanna. Before her, he smoked twenty or more a day, mostly while he was drinking but she'd made it a condition of their relationship that he stopped. He'd done it, not for his health, he'd done it for her, going cold turkey over a long weekend during which she was always at his side, plying him with coffee, movies and sex. It had been a pretty good way to put the habit to rest he had to admit.

The temptation was always there of course, especially over a beer or coffee, or while driving but of late it had faded. This was the first time he'd succumbed and he had no clear idea as to why it had happened, or why he'd not thrown the packet away already; his mind slid away and rebelled every time he thought about it. He knew Joanna would be displeased and probably angry enough to break things off but somehow the thought hadn't been strong enough to stop his mouth working faster than his brain back at the Clarenville service station. It was as if his critical faculties had been suspended at exactly the right moment and only for long enough for an old vice to resurface.

I don't need them.

It was his mantra the last time he'd quit. It was going to have to be again.

Besides, after the two smokes, the urge abated and by the time he was upstairs readying for bed he decided he was definitely, finally, for sure done with the Marlboro and he'd dispose of the rest in the morning.

It was his last coherent thought for a while. His head hit the pillow and he went off, like a switch had been flipped, down into sleep.

His dreams were fractured and confused; green leaves and black threads, laughing Irishmen, songs and drums and snatches of song and verse and a definite sense of searching for something long lost, almost tangible but always out of reach. He woke in darkness at three in the morning, not quite refreshed but not ready to fall back into the same disconcerting dreamscape.

He watched shadows and light roll across the ceiling as the thin nighttime traffic passed on the road outside. Every headlight beam cast the shadow of the big trees outside across the room. The branches danced, the leaves fluttered. Keith thought about black tracery and cold wood inside a gaping wound and all desire to sleep left him.

I want a smoke.

He pushed the thought away. He got up, padded through to the kitchen and got the coffee machine going before switching on his laptop. He meant to check his email to see if there was any news of Gerry from the Professor but when the machine came on it was still sitting at the diary page where he'd left off from it.

Maybe it'll help stop me from thinking about the smokes.

He fetched a mug of coffee and resumed reading.

"July 5th

"I have written before in these pages about my lack of faith in the spiritual. I grew up with too many nuns and priests trying to hammer it into me. It nearly worked for a while but to have everything you have ever loved taken from you despite all your prayers and entreaties goes a long way to making any belief in a higher power seem futile. If there is a God I have been so angry with him for so long that if I ever meet him I will tell him to go to Hell, for it is no more than he deserves.

"And yet, tonight here in the lonely dark I find myself wishing for some of the simple belief my own mother took for granted, giving her peace at the end, a peace I could never find but would wish for my men here in the camp. I have come to believe they might need it after the events of this day.

"Murphy is dead.

"He went in his sleep in the early hours of this morning, which was a blessing for he had woken after midnight in pain the like of which no man should be asked to suffer. He could scarcely move beyond shaking his head from side to side. He did so in such a frenzy, I thought he might break his neck; if he had managed it, it might have been a mercy.

"He pleaded long and loud for either Kelly or myself to put him out of his misery but, cowards that we are, we did not even give him that much peace. At the end the creeping thing in his blood crawled all across his torso, legs and arms. We poured as much uisque into him as he could take and sent him down into a stupor from which he thankfully never returned. He passed between one breath and the next.

"Kelly and I together decided we could not allow the others to see the state of him, for it would have meant a mutiny from which our venture here would never recover. So, we wrapped him in three layers of blankets from the store, leaving only his face exposed and put him lying out in state in the main cabin. I have cause for concern in having even that much of him exposed, for there is no sign of a peaceful passing in his features, contorted as they are in pain, even in death.

"But it is the least I can do for him.

"We had a sending off for him, if you can call the mournful silence we suffered any kind of wake at all. The uisque took a hammering all round and I confess to partaking of my fair share of it, for Murphy was a good worker, a better man and his humor and company will be sorely missed by us all.

"I set three men to digging a grave, although in this ground, it will be a wet one. But we shall put him to his final rest tomorrow and I shall say the necessary words. I will even try to believe them, for the time it takes to give him peace.

"It is all I can do for him now. It is all any of us can do."

"July 6th

"I gave the crew a day's rest from working at the face to properly mourn poor Murphy's passing but in hindsight it might have been for the best to keep them working. Malone, never one to miss an opportunity to further himself, has not been slow to blame me for the death. Even while we were still planting poor Murphy in the ground, Malone said I was not a friend of the Wee Folk, which is perfectly true but the manner in which he said it was designed solely to turn the men against me.

"If he had spoken out anywhere but at the graveside, I would have knocked him on his arse. It might well come to that pass, sooner rather than later, for Malone has achieved his purpose. I see it in the eyes of the crew, good Catholics to a man during the day and superstitious idolaters as soon as it gets dark. It is a bad combination, even more so in such an isolated community as we are.

"I have thought of sending someone out to fetch a priest, one who might administer to this frightened flock. But anyone I send might take it into his head to keep walking and never return. I know I would, given money in my pocket and half a chance of escape. So, I have kept my peace, for now, although my own temper has grown foul and must be kept in check at all times lest I do something I will regret at penniless leisure.

"The uisque and ale flowed freely again today and loosened tongues that might otherwise have stayed silent. I learned the men are as worried as I have been about our prospects in this place. If we had not all sunk everything we have into the venture, I do believe there would be a consensus to turn about and take our chances elsewhere, even though we all know only the poorhouse or starvation wait along that particular road.

"I learned something else too, something not brought to my attention until now, as the men believed my tending to poor Murphy should take precedence. There have been even more of those blasted wood dolls found, hiding in plain sight all around the camp, in the rafters of the cabin and stores, even turning up sitting on the end of the bunks in the morning. And still not a man will admit to their manufacture, all swearing blind their innocence.

"Malone, of course, has suggested these too are the work of the bloody Wee Folk and some, if not all, of the men are inclined to agree with him. But one of those men is obviously, to my mind at least, the culprit.

"Someone is lying to me and in the name of the Lord they swear by, when I find out which of them that is, I shall lay them out on their arse alongside Malone."

Keith looked up, his concentration broken by a sudden sound in the apartment, a rustling, like crumpled paper unfolding. He sat, sipping at coffee going cold through neglect, waiting to see if the sound would be repeated. It was an old apartment though; and up here on the top of the building, in a windy city, the creaky timbers, rumbling pipes and loose shingles came with the package.

There was no sound now, not even of traffic outside, into the dead hours of the night when everything in the city fell still.

After a minute or so he went back to his reading.

"July 7th

"Murphy's death has cast a pall over our endeavors hanging as low as the dank clouds and swarms of black flies that have plagued us these past few days. I see the same misery in the men's eyes I feel in my own heart and there is a sense of foreboding, a feeling the worst of our trials still lie ahead of us.

"It does not help it has been another bad day at the face. What little silver we have garnered so far proves to be all the rock is prepared to yield. The men were tardy in starting this morning, which I put down, at first, to the uisque and ale they had consumed. But I found out they had another matter on their mind.

"The first man on site after breaking fast discovered three more of the damned wood dolls sitting at the shaft entrance, as if blocking his way. And three more were found in shaft two, arranged around the dark pool in the bottom level. I have ordered each and every one of the things to be cast into the stove, along with every one that might be found from this moment on.

"Malone, of course, let it be known to anyone that would listen that I would only succeed in calling down mischief and wrath on our heads but I will have no more truck with this superstitious shite. My future is at stake here and that of all these men. Even if they do not know it, I am responsible for their wellbeing in this place and there is nothing I take more seriously. I only wish I could get them to understand this simple, uncomplicated fact.

"If that were the sum total of my worries, it would be enough for sure but there is an even more grave concern now, one that has me fearful not only for my long-term fate but for my chances of even seeing out these next few days to come.

"Murphy may have only been the first of many, mayhap the first of us all.

"Kelly, who did such a sterling job of looking after Murphy in his last hours, came to me while the men were at supper and I was here in the storeroom taking inventory. I knew immediately by the look in his eyes it was trouble we did not need.

"'I have something to show you. And you are not going to like it,' he said.

"And he was right. He rolled up his left sleeve. There, faint but most definite, all the way up the inside of his forearm, ran a tracery of black. The infection coursed in the man's veins.

"'It is the same?' I asked but I did not need to; all I needed was the evidence of my own eyes. 'What can be done?'

"But Kelly merely shook his head and said nothing. We have no doctor out here save Kelly and if he was at a loss as to how the contagion might be prevented, then how am I, a simple miner from Dublin, going to be able to do better?

"We have sat together these past hours, passing a bottle of uisque between us and reminiscing about the auld country and better days. I sensed a great weariness and no little despair in the man as he took his leave to head off to bed. He showed me his arm again as he stood. The veins are blacker already and although they have not yet spread above his elbow it is surely only a matter of time.

"I will check on him again first thing in the morning but for now, as soon as I finish this sentence, I shall go and inspect my own arms and legs. If I find any trace of the black these might be the last words I commit to paper for I will not go hard, not like Murphy went. I do not have it in me to endure such a fate.

"I would rather take a bullet."

The parallels were too strong to ignore. Something had got into the miners and chances were the same thing had gotten Gerry; and it might well be contagious.

Keith's concentration blew away. He stood, almost too fast and already stripping off his clothes headed for the shower where he scrubbed and scrubbed under scalding hot water. The old plumbing rattled and clanked and complained but Keith kept scrubbing until his skin was red and the heat got too much for him to stand.

After washing he checked his skin again, closely, studying arms and legs for any sign of puncture wounds. He found a couple of minor scratches and even they caused panic to rise back up, threatening to have him hyperventilating. He checked both arms, both legs, even tried to check his back in the small mirror over the hand-basin but there was no sign of any black tracery.

Not yet.

He headed back through to the kitchen. He made another pot of coffee and this time added a large slug of dark rum to it. The warmth as it spread through his system did a lot to calm any fraying nerves he had. But he wasn't ready to read any farther in the diary. If the disease, contagion, whatever the hell it was, did spread among the miners back then, it wasn't something he needed to know about right here, all alone in the night in a quiet apartment.

Except it wasn't as quiet as he might hope. Now he'd stopped moving around and sat at the table with his rum-infused coffee he heard it again, the same as before, the faintest of rustles. Now it didn't sound like paper, more like dried leaves being crunched together.

There it was again, louder this time, as if his taking note of it had made it bolder. Keith got up and checked the kitchen first, looking in cupboards, under chairs, even in the fridge but he couldn't pinpoint the source of the noise. As he walked toward the main living area it got louder again.

He checked everywhere, behind the bookshelves, under the sofa, looked down inside the two large, ugly flower vases Joanna had inherited from a dead Aunt. Still he couldn't find it, although the noise was definitely louder here and growing more insistent.

Finally, by turning his head from side to side and keeping still, he was able to get a better bead on it; it originated in the direction of the picture window looking out over the courtyard where he'd had his earlier smokes.

He walked over and looked out and down. The yard wasn't well lit but he hadn't put the room light on and there were no reflections to interfere with his view. Even then, at first all he saw was the dark shadows under the tall birch tree. Then he caught a movement on the trunk, fast and fluid, coming up fast from ground level.

It moved so quick he wasn't sure he'd seen it, until the noise came again and a pair of fiery, tiny emerald eyes at his own eye level looked straight at him from deep within the branches of the tree.

6

Gerry woke again, out of soft green dreams into the same locked-in nightmare.

It was night now, or so he guessed; the window blinds were closed and the overhead light glared, far too bright. He had been left sitting up in the bed and the dialysis machine kept up its monotonous beat at his left. The draining sensation felt as bad as ever, as if he was constantly taking a leak but at least the itch in his arm had faded to pins-and-needles tingling. His throat was dry, his head felt light and he couldn't feel much of anything below the waist.

But I'm alive. Or at least, I think I am.

His mom sat in the bedside chair, reading a book. He stared at her hands and the zone of flesh showing between wrist and forearm but he saw no trace of black in the veins.

Mom? Are you okay?

He got confirmation of his paralysis as soon as he spoke; he was still locked inside his body. His mom didn't show any sign of having heard him.

But something else had woken at his call. He wasn't alone, there was something inside with him. He heard it louder now, creeping, rustling as it grew and sent out new filaments. There was a good reason he couldn't move his body; he was a safe place, a piece of immobile warm meat that would serve perfectly as a host. He saw it in his mind's eye, the mannequin taking shape inside him, not flesh in there anymore but a solid, unwieldy mass of twigs and branches and buds, a sculpture waiting to be born when the meat and tissue finally succumbed.

As if it had been emboldened by the thought he felt it swelling inside him, a brick in his stomach that quickly became a cramp knotting his guts.

Well that's great. On top of everything else I get to shit myself.

Whatever it was sitting there, it wasn't intent on going down, although it was definitely intent on coming out. It climbed. He felt it scrape in his esophagus, tasted blood at the back of his throat, felt his inner surfaces rip and tear as wood and twig grabbed hold to pull itself up and out of him.

He screamed in a wail; the sound echoed long and loud in his skull. His mom kept reading.

The thump and thud of the dialysis machine got slowly faster, the beat ramping up in time with his heart as whatever was coming reached his throat. He felt it scrambling frantically, tearing at his tonsils and the root of his tongue as it looked for a hold. He tasted more blood and would have gagged if he'd been able to move. All he could do was endure as it kept coming, faster now, as if it knew it was close to escape.

The pressure grew almost unbearable as it stretched his jaw as wide as it would open and scratched at his tongue, heaving the rest of itself out of his throat and into his mouth. He heard wood scrape across his teeth, felt it scratch inside his lips, looking for a hold. More blood now and a dry, acrid taste of vinegar and burnt oil.

Then it was all there, forcing its way out in a bloody spray. The white of his gown spotted with red as the wood and twig and branches writhed and took form. He looked down his nose and saw it coming.

The head and shoulders of a small, all too familiar mannequin crawled out of his mouth. Gerry felt its legs tickle his palate then it was free. It rolled forward, falling into his lap and leaving a trail of blood and slime all down his front behind it. It lay there in a bloody heap, the twigs slowly intertwining as if it was catching its breath.

The dialysis machine thudded and whined and Gerry's mom finally looked round, put her book down and stood.

"Gerry? It's mom. Can you hear me?"

She bent to look in Gerry's eyes. At the same time the

wooden doll in Gerry's lap stood up and looked around, a curious new thing in a new place.

Get away, mom. Get away.

She went to the door and shouted.

"Get a doctor. I think he is waking up this time."

Before his mom turned away from the door the small wooden doll walked across the bed sheet to the right leaving a trail of tiny footprints. It jumped down off the bed and out of Gerry's sight.

Mom, watch out!

This time she did move, reacting as if struck.

She was at the side of the bed again in an instant, taking his hand in hers.

"Come on, darling. Come back to us."

Mom?

"Don't try to talk, take it easy. The doctor's on his way."

Tears welled at the corners of her eyes, setting him off too, into violent sobs he couldn't control. When she reached over to hug him close, his arms came up to draw her in and when she pulled away and called for a doctor again, he was able to pull fully upright against the pillows at his back. He looked down at his gown. There was no blood spattered across his lap, no tiny footprints on the sheets.

And I'm awake. I'm finally awake. It was all a bad dream.

Suddenly the room filled up, his parents, his doctor and two nurses, in a flurry of activity.

A small voice, singing softly in an Irish lilt, rose from somewhere below the bed.

My Bonnie lies over the ocean,

My Bonnie lies over the sea.

My Bonnie lies over the ocean.

Oh bring back my Bonnie to me.

If anyone but Gerry heard it, they showed no sign of it.

7

Keith was still sitting in the main room with the lights out when Joanna got in from her shift after eight. He'd hardly taken his gaze off the birch tree for hours, not even after the sun came up. There had been no more sounds, no more sightings of the emerald eyes but he was done with sleep for the night and he'd sat up sipping rum and watching but the show was over. He had a feeling he'd seen exactly what something had intended him to see; it had announced its presence, letting him know it was there.

But what is it? Was it a warning or a hello? And what happens next?

"You haven't been up all night drinking, have you?" she said when he went through to the hallway to meet her, still with the glass in his hand.

"Only a small one. I couldn't sleep," he replied. "Too much excitement yesterday." He tried for a smile but she wasn't buying it.

"You look like shit. Are you going in this morning?"

"Yeah, the Professor will be expecting me. I'll try to get off early and get a nap in later this afternoon. Then we'll talk about the wedding, the baby and stuff. I promise."

She gave him a peck on the cheek. For a second he thought she might smell smoke on him again but he got away with it, this time.

He made breakfast for them both while Joanna had a shower; a couple of slices of buttered toast and some milk for her, as she'd be heading straight to bed and black coffee and a bagel for him. What he wanted was more rum, a bucketful of the stuff but as he'd told Joanna, the Professor would be expecting him this morning; there would be work to do on the finds they'd brought back. And maybe there would be good news about Gerry.

Joanna was quiet while eating.

"Tough shift?" he asked.

"Dead baby," she replied. She didn't have to say anything else. He knew she'd process it in her own way, she always did. It came with the job but it didn't mean she had to like it.

"Look, I don't have to go in for a couple of hours yet, if you want to talk?"

"No, it's okay. I'll sleep. I need to sleep."

He left with a promise they'd have time for a talk before she had to go back out in the evening.

He lit up a smoke as soon as he was out of sight of any of the apartment windows.

The Professor was out in the corridor by the coffee machine when Keith arrived. His hair was unruly, he hadn't shaved and he had a bleary-eyed look Keith had seen already this morning in his own bathroom mirror.

"Bad night, Professor?"

"I couldn't sleep," the older man replied. "I kept thinking about poor Gerry and about what I've read in the bloody diary. In a way I wish we'd never found it."

"I read some more of it last night," Keith said.

The Professor looked into Keith's eyes.

"How far did you get this time?"

"Murphy's dead, Kelly's infected..."

The Professor interrupted him.

"And the twig mannequins are turning up all over the camp. I remember. You've a bit to go yet then. But there's something I need to show you."

The Professor took his coffee from the machine and led Keith along to his office two doors down.

"Any news on Gerry?" Keith asked.

"He's awake," the Professor said. "And it sounds like they've controlled the infection, disease, whatever the hell it is. They're holding him for observation for a few days, to be on the safe side."

"Well, that's good news."

The Professor opened the office door and showed Keith inside.

"It's not Gerry I'm worried about. It's me. Where did this come from?"

At first Keith didn't know what the Professor meant. Then his gaze fell on the Professor's desk. The figure was about ten inches tall, made of tangled twig and foliage and sat on the edge of the desk, as if caught in the act of swinging its legs. Keith walked around to look into what should be its face.

If it had stared at him with green, flashing eyes right then he'd have been out of the door and gone, never to return, but there were only dark, empty sockets. It was what it appeared to be, a greenery-coated mannequin sculpted from fresh growth wood, with the foliage starting to yellow at the edges.

"This is a joke, right?" Keith asked.

"I'm not laughing," the Professor replied. "I thought it must have come with us from the site and maybe one of the two other lads left it as a prank. But my door has been locked all night, I've got the only key apart from the watchman and I doubt this is his handwork."

"Maybe it did come with us from the site," Keith replied. "We were all tired yesterday and…"

"I was tired, not blind," the Professor replied. His voice descended to a whisper. "I think it's all happening again, here as it did then."

"What, the infection?" Instinctively, Keith checked his hands for signs of the black tracery.

"No," the Professor said and he suddenly looked much older than his age and tired enough to keel over at any moment. "That's only the start. Finish reading the diary; you need to do it anyway. Go and finish it now and then we'll talk."

As Keith turned to leave the Professor picked up the wood mannequin and dropped it unceremoniously in his wastebasket.

"And if any more of these buggers turn up, let me know immediately."

Keith went through the adjoining door leading to the workroom cum lab, his home away from home during term time. The gear and boxes of samples from their trip were still stacked to one side and he knew he'd have to tackle that, sooner rather than later. It wasn't only the Professor's urging that made him get out the laptop and make a restart on the diary; it was the thought of those flashing green eyes in the dark. If there was an answer in the diary he had to know and he had to know now.

"July 8th

"A bad week is growing worse by the day and I know not if I will be able to face any more. Mayhap writing about matters here will ease my fraying nerves and make me brave. But strange things are abroad this night. I have closed the door firmly and taken to the uisque for comfort. For the moment it suffices, but only for the moment.

"Kelly has gone missing. His absence was noted at breakfast and at first little was made of it, for the man was known to take a stroll along the pond after rising. But when he had not returned in time for his shift at the face I sent two men along the pond to look for him, worried that he might have succumbed to his infection and be lying somewhere unable to call for help.

"But no sign of him was found. His bedroll is by his bunk and his box of personal belongings is here in this storeroom; I can see it from where I sit, so it is unlikely he has taken off for more civilized company. Knowing what I do of the man I can only assume he has chosen to flee for fear of passing the black tracery on to the rest of us.

"I am sorely vexed and fearful it is already too late and the contagion might even now be in all of us but as I am the only man here privy to the information Kelly was infected I think it for the best to hold my peace.

"Peace seems to be something Malone is determined to avoid if he can help it. He has tried to use Kelly's absence to further stir up the men, even going so far as to be suggesting the Wee Folk have abducted him as punishment for my skepticism. Thankfully several of the crew berated him for talking pish and shite, which saved me from having to put down any rebellion. But the mood is darkening in the men by the hour and every

THE GREEN AND THE BLACK

chip away at the work face revealing only more of the dark gray stone and no sign of the silver is another blow to their morale.

"It does not help matters that the blasted twig dolls keep appearing wherever you look, although no one has yet seen one being put in place and still no one will admit to the making of them. Seeing a serried rank of them along the side of the pond as I made my inspection before retiring tonight broke the last vestige of the control I have been maintaining on my temper.

"A black rage came on me and I cursed, stomped and kicked at the damned things until there was nothing left but broken twig and crushed leaves floating in scummy filth on top of the water. It did much to improve my mood but such a relative peace of mind proved to be short-lived.

"As I walked back toward the camp, my inspection complete, I heard soft singing, as if coming from a distance. At first, I thought it to be the men, raising their own spirits in a song in the cabin. But this was not coming from the camp; it came from the shafts in the rock face.

"Bring back, bring back, oh bring back my bonnie to me, to me.

"My first thought was it must be poor Kelly, mayhap having stumbled and become lost in the dark of the mine, now raving in his sickness. But as I got closer I realized the singing voice came in a high pitched, broad Irish accent that did not come from the throat of any man I knew.

"Bring back, bring back, oh bring back my bonnie to me, to me.

"My legs threatened to betray me, going weak and trembling as if I had walked too many miles but I forced myself onward, for Kelly's sake.

"I reached the mouth of shaft one, barely able to see in the dark, the mine ahead merely a deeper patch of blackness in the shadows. The singing was louder now.

"Bring back, bring back, oh bring back my bonnie to me, to me.

"Suddenly I was no longer so sure in my skepticism and Malone's tales of Wee Folk and bogles did not seem so outlandish as they had in the warmth and light of the cabin.

"'Kelly? It's Donnelly. Are you hurt, man?'

"I called out, just in case, although I knew in my heart this was none of Kelly's doing. The singing stopped and I had the strangest feeling I had been noticed and there was someone there inside the mine mouth, watching and waiting to see what manner of action I might take.

"As for myself I had already decided on my course; no amount of silver or uisque could impel me to enter the dark mineshaft right then.

"I backed away slowly, not wishing to draw further attention to myself. At the last as I turned away I thought I caught sight of something, the merest hint of color, green and flashing like emeralds in the dark but when I looked again there was nothing but the black.

"As I walked back toward the camp as fast as I was able without either giving away my terror or breaking into a run the singing followed me.

"Bring back, bring back, oh bring back my bonnie to me, to me."

Keith had to sit back from the laptop; his hands shook and his heartbeat was up, as if he too had been there in the dark with the foreman, hearing the song, seeing the green eyes. He remembered the Professor's words from earlier.

"I think it's happening again, here as it did then."

8

Since waking up Gerry felt fine, physically at least. Mentally was another matter. The strange birth of the mannequin from within his body was too vivid, too real for him to easily dismiss it as a dream.

But what else could it be. There was no blood, no footprints.

There had been the singing. As he sat up in the bed he tried to believe the song had been a fading echo, the last of the nightmare following him into wakefulness. He'd had nightmares before, plenty of them as a kid, usually brought on by reading too late into the night; Morlocks under the bed, Gollum in a dark corner, the bogeyman in the closet. They were long in the past.

Or so I thought.

He wondered whether it might be the drugs he'd been given but the high strangeness had begun before he even got to the hospital. Somehow everything was linked to the black liquor in the old bottle and his out of character decision to drink from it. That's where the answer lay.

But what, if anything, can I do about it?

Then there was his mom and the nurse. If it hadn't all been a dream then they too might be infected. Was some other wooden abomination even now growing inside them? It wasn't anything he could explain to his mother; he couldn't even begin to imagine broaching that particular conversation with either parent.

But perhaps the nurse might understand?

He tried the first chance he got, the next time she came in to check up on him. He waited until she'd checked his needle entry points before he spoke.

"Should you be so close to me without some kind of protective mask or gloves?" he said. "You don't know what I have, do you?"

She smiled.

"The doctor thinks you had a bacterial infection and we've flushed it all out of you. Besides, we're all having our blood-work checked, in case it's something hiding deep. We might not know what you had but we'll know it if we see it under the scope."

"Mom and dad too?"

She smiled again. He looked into her eyes but saw no black tracery.

"Yes, your parents too. We're testing everybody you've been in contact with. We've even been trying to get in touch with all of the people who brought you in. We finally got someone at the University and your professor says he'll make sure everybody gets tested. The good news is that none of your friends appears to have any symptoms; with such a severe case as you had, we'd expect any cross contamination to be showing up by now if it were ever going to show up."

Gerry felt something come loose in his chest, relief easing a tension he hadn't known was there.

"And I'm free of it?"

"As far as we can tell. This morning's blood-work came back clear, the cellulose build-up has stopped, the darkness has gone from your circulatory system and you're awake and lucid. I'd call it a win, wouldn't you?"

"But how did I get cellulose in my blood cells in the first place? I'm not a bloody Triffid."

The reference went straight over her head and she didn't reply but she did smile again as she turned to leave.

"Try to relax. We hope to get all these needles out of you later today and see about helping you get back on your feet. Until then, chill."

He managed a smile of his own in reply. But after she'd gone and he was once again alone in the room, the memories preyed on him, of the taste of dry wood and leaves in his mouth and the tearing sensation as the thing climbed out of him. He still tasted the blood at the back of his throat.

If it were a dream, surely it would have faded by now?

Gerry rarely remembered his dreams these days, only snatches and fragments. For something to be so vivid, in full, wide-screen color, taste and smell-o-vision, was unheard of.

And surely no coincidence?

He wondered if the team had uncovered anything back at the site to throw light on his predicament, then remembered the nurse saying they'd been contacted back at University.

They've gone home. I should call them.

He'd looked around the room and seen no sight of his tablet, or of his clothes for that matter. There was a small bedside cabinet to his right but the tubes and machines he was hooked up to prevented him from leaning over to check what was in it. He resolved to ask his mom for his tablet when she next came in.

All such thoughts disappeared as soon as he saw her.

She arrived in the doorway not long after the nurse had gone.

She looked like she had wood running not only through her veins but under her skin, twig and branch and root in a clotted mass, wriggling over and around each other like worms in a feeding frenzy. She walked across the room in a stiff-legged gait, as if her legs had gone solid. Gerry backed away as she reached a hand for him; her fingernails looked sharp and glossy like thick black thorns.

"Are you okay, sweetheart?" she said. She sounded like mom all right and she acted as if there was nothing untoward, as if she was completely unaware of her appearance.

I'm hallucinating again. This is another weird after effect of the sickness

He didn't believe it. He could only stare, unable to say anything meaningful as she sat in the chair by his side and opened a book. The profile view of her face was hardly any better; her skin seethed, rising and falling as stem and branch grew in and around the jaw and cheekbones. Her lips moved; it was an old habit she always had when reading but at the same time Gerry was horrified to see a bulge grow in her throat, a wriggling, struggling bulge, something climbing up, trying to get out.

"Mom," he said, far too loud. She must have heard something of his terror in his voice. She turned, the concern obvious in her eyes.

"What is it, darling?"

He tried to speak but could only watch as the squirming mass moved higher up his mom's throat. A branch with five tiny twigs on the end emerged from her mouth and grabbed at the corner of her lips. She coughed and blood dripped down her front, spattered her book but she didn't seem to notice, even as the mannequin appeared, head first, torso and legs following in a mess of bloody slime. It slithered, all the way down her blouse to lie, panting between the pages of the book.

Finally, Gerry screamed, thrashing his arms so hard he tugged one of the IV tubes loose. Blood spurted at the crook of his elbow. His mom stood. Her book and the thing on it, slid to the floor. Gerry heard small footsteps, scuttling away.

"Nurse!" his mom shouted.

She leaned over him, drools of blood and spit still dripping from her mouth, the rustling foliage inside her still squirming and weaving its way through her body.

Gerry screamed again as she reached for him.

The nurse arrived. She had black veins running all the way through her arms and up her neck where he could see above her scrubs. A small bloody wood and leaf mannequin sat on her shoulder and blood ran all down the front of her scrubs. The mannequin waved at Gerry with one long hand, then swung, shoulder to breast pocket to pants pocket and down the leg to the floor where it too scuttled away.

Gerry's screams subsided to sobbing as he tried to back away, only to be stopped by the hard frame of the bed behind him.

The nurse got a fresh IV into him and the sedative washed through him almost immediately, sending him quickly down to a sea of green foliage, swirling and seething, branch and twig and leaf, going yellow at the edges.

He fell into it and was swallowed whole. As he went down

he heard the song again. There were three voices now and they all sounded happy.

"Bring back, bring back, oh bring back my bonnie to me, to me."

9

Keith left the lab and went outside for a smoke. He was down to his last two so he only had one of them despite a now constant craving.

Make it last. I'm not buying any more. I don't need them. It's the blasted diary's fault; I need to calm down.

The flashing emerald eyes he'd seen in the tree the night before were big in his mind, along with the black tracery covering Gerry's arms. Keith had compulsively checked his own hands and forearms every five minutes for most of the morning and he did so again after grinding out the butt of the smoke, pushing his cuffs as far back as they would go to expose the inside of his wrists.

I'm still all clear. But for how long?

When he went back upstairs, the Professor was waiting for him at the top of the stairwell.

"I thought you'd got stopped with those cancer sticks? You shouldn't let whatever's going on here force you back into bad habits."

Keith almost told him about the green eyes in the dark but kept quiet. There was too much high weirdness around already without adding to it. Besides, the Professor had already moved on.

"Do you know where we can find the other two lads? We need to get some tests done at St. Clare's, blood work mainly, to clear us. They know we're coming."

"This request came from Gander?"

"Yes," the Professor replied. "It looks like Gerry's on the mend but they want to make sure, I guess."

"I'll give the lads a call," Keith said, taking out his cell-phone.

Neither of the students answered at the other end. He left a voice mail message for both of them before turning back to the Professor, who looked worried.

"I don't think we can afford to miss these tests," he said. "The doctor in Gander was pretty insistent and if what's in the diary is true, he's right to be worried."

If the Professor thought it was serious, it was time Keith paid closer attention.

"I know where their flat is," Keith replied. "If they've not come in yet, they're probably still in bed. We can go and pick them up. You got your car today?"

The Professor nodded.

Keith went quickly along to the lab and put his laptop in his knapsack; he might need it for diversion if there was to be a long wait at the hospital.

"Come on then. You drive, I'll give directions and we can all head up to the hospital together."

Keith had only been to the students' apartment once, for a pretty riotous party for Bill's twentieth birthday. It was downtown and they had an attic flat in what had once been a large townhouse but was now converted into six tiny student apartments, a conversion resulting in an easy money earner for the landlord. Keith recognized him when he answered their ring of the doorbell; the older man had been in and out of the apartment on party night, trying to keep the noise down.

"We're here to see Bill and Doug, top floor?"

The man grunted.

"Go on up. I think they're still in bed. They were up late partying by the sound of it, all kinds of stomping about and yelling. Only went quiet about two."

Keith went first up the stairs with the Professor following right behind; the landlord didn't bother following them. By the time they reached the top floor everything had fallen still; if the lads had been noisy the night before they were making up for it now. Keith rapped hard on the apartment door.

"Doug, Bill? It's Keith and the Professor I need to talk to you. It's important."

There was no answer, not even when Keith knocked harder a second time.

"Do you think they've gone out?" the Professor asked.

"The guy downstairs would have told us," Keith replied. "I'm not giving up yet."

He tried the door, more in hope than anything and was surprised when the handle turned easily. The door swung open onto an empty hallway beyond.

"Doug? Bill? Anybody home?"

There was still no reply. Keith, with the Professor following, stepped inside and closed the main door behind them. Neither of them spoke. A silence hung in the air that felt like it shouldn't be broken.

The apartment was made up of four tiny rooms. The main living area and kitchenette would have told anyone visiting that students lived here, with discarded beer bottles and fast food boxes littering both on and below the coffee table and a thin layer of grease coating the work surfaces. There was a powered-up laptop on one of the few clear spots on the kitchen table but there was no sign of the lads.

They kept looking. The first door was the lavatory and shower area; the small, cramped, room looked like it needed an industrial cleaning but again it too was empty. That left two other doors, to the two bedrooms.

Both the doors were shut and Keith was suddenly loath to enter, dreading what he might find. He was thinking about the diary and the story of the contagion.

Murphy went hard at the end.

He hoped the lads were sleeping off a drunk.

"Doug? Bill?" he called out again.

He got only silence in reply. He put out a hand to the nearest door handle, then paused.

"What do you think?" he whispered to the Professor

"They might be sick. We need to find them."

The Professor had whispered back in return; neither of them was keen on breaking the silence. The thought of one, or even both, of the lads lying unconscious the way Gerry had been when they got him to the hospital was enough to get Keith moving. He turned the handle and stepped into the nearer of the two rooms.

A cell-phone sat on the bedside table. Keith guessed that if he checked he'd find his own earlier voicemail waiting there. A figure was bundled under the covers, completely swaddled.

"Bill? Come on, lad. Wake up. We need to talk."

Keith stepped over and pushed the figure at the shoulder. Instead of meeting a firm body his hand kept going; whatever was underneath it felt too soft, not like flesh. He pulled the covers away.

Black, empty eye sockets stared up at him from an intricately woven head, nothing but twig and branch and foliage, going slightly yellow at the edges.

Two seconds later Keith was back out in the hallway, trying to remember how to breathe. The Professor took him by the shoulders and looked into his eyes then tried to look past him into the bedroom. Keith moved to block the older man's view but the Professor had already guessed what was there.

"It's another bloody mannequin, isn't it? It's like it said in the journal. It's what's left after the infection has run its course."

Keith sobbed, nearly laughed.

"Don't talk rubbish, Professor There's nothing in there about people turning to mannequins. Not in any bit I've read."

The Professor looked grim but determined.

"I told you; you need to read it to the end. Come on. We better check the other lad."

Keith held back.

"You do it. I don't think I can look again, not yet."

It only took the Professor seconds to step into the other room and back out again. A slight nod was all he needed to make.

Neither of the students was here. In their place were two, life-size wood and twig mannequins. Whether this was the result of some conversion process, or whether it was some kind of joke, Keith didn't care. He needed to get out of here and he needed to get out now.

They didn't speak again until they were back out at the car.

"You think that was them?" he asked.

The Professor nodded.

"What's left of them anyway. It's either that or believe the same artist did the work at the miners' camp and followed us here to do this. It might be more logical but less believable, if you see what I mean?"

"We need to tell somebody," Keith said.

"Who would you suggest?" the older man replied. "I've been thinking about it. The cops won't believe us, not when they see what's lying in the beds. A student prank is how they'll see this one, at the start at least. By the time they begin to take anything seriously it'll be too late."

"Maybe it is a prank," Keith said. "Maybe..."

The Professor shook his head.

"Read to the end of the journal. Then think over everything that's happened. Like me, you'll come to the only conclusion possible."

"Which is?"

"Read it, Keith. But I think you know already. And first, we need to get ourselves to the hospital and get those blood tests done. I have no intention of turning into a fucking bush in my sleep."

Hearing his fear made vocal in such blunt words suddenly brought everything into focus for Keith.

"You're right, hospital it is. But I hate leaving the lads in the apartment. Surely there's somebody we can tell, somebody who can do something?"

"Nobody will believe us. This is too far out into the Twilight Zone for rational explanation. I think we're on our own."

"So, what do we do?"

"Hospital first. We need to make sure we're actually going to be around to do anything at all."

Keith kept quiet on the short trip to the hospital. Questions were futile. The Professor knew only as much as Keith did apart from the bit about the journal and the older man was pretty adamant he wasn't going to discuss it until they'd both read it all the way through.

He didn't get a chance to catch up on his reading at the hospital. Minutes after announcing themselves at the main reception area they were called up to a small third floor room. A calm, efficient nurse took almost a pint of blood from each of them, collecting it in separate sample tubes, labeled as heading to different labs for testing. She also took thin shavings of skin samples from the ball of Keith's thumb.

After the blood work came head and chest X-Rays.

"What are you looking for?" Keith asked the nurse.

"We've been told it's some kind of rapid clotting agent. We need to make sure your circulatory system is clear of blockages."

Yeah, that's probably a good idea.

While he was stripped for the X-Ray, Keith again gave his exposed skin a once over. He was pale, probably a bit too much so but there was no sign of any dark tracery. It got him thinking about the two young students taken in their sleep and the green-eyed thing outside his window. It was going to be a long time before he'd be able to lie down in a bed.

After the X-Ray, he thought they'd be allowed to leave but they were asked to stay on by the doctor in charge of their procedures.

"We've got some slides being made up in Microscopy of your skin samples. I want to take a look at them first before we let you walk away."

Keith saw the look in the man's eyes and made an educated guess.

"It's Gerry, isn't it? He's not as well as we've been told, is he?"

"He's recovering, physically at least. But there appears to be some mental degradation. It has his doctors in Gander worried. We want to make sure we don't miss anything at this end before letting you out into the general population."

Keith showed the doctor his arms.

"Look, all clear," he said.

"It's what we can't see that worries us," the doctor replied and herded Keith into a small waiting room, where the Professor was already sitting, reading a six-month-old Auto magazine with no apparent sign of interest.

"You need to work on your bedside manner," Keith said but the doctor had already gone.

For the first hour he expected to be told at any minute they could go but after a while he realized they were in for a longish wait. He tried fetching coffee from the nearest vending machine but it tasted as bad as the stuff back at the faculty and smelled even worse. Neither of them drank much more than a sip. The Professor put his head back and within minutes had fallen into a deep sleep.

Keith envied him the ability. The idea of twig and branch burrowing its way through him in a dark room made him want to scream and the urge for a cigarette grew strong again.

He tried to fight off the inevitable by firing up his laptop. Within seconds he'd found his place in the journal and was transported back to the long-ago group of miners, a group he was feeling closer to by the minute.

"July 10th
"I scarcely know where to begin to tally the misfortunes of this day. All I know is it has sealed my fate and made me rethink my relationship with my creator. If there is a God, his mercy may be the only way for me to meet my beloved in the hereafter and if there is a chance of that, however slight, I have no problem with being a hypocrite on my deathbed.

"But more anon, for I have much to relate while I am still able to write.

"The day began badly, a portent of what was to come. Kelly has not returned and I am coming to believe we shall never see the man again. His prolonged absence has been noted among the men and although I have said nothing, it has not prevented gossip and rumor from circulating.

"Even at breakfast I could tell the mood of the crew was bad. They were surly and disrespectful for the most part and Malone had a smirk on his gob making me think he had been agitating them again behind my back. I was to find it to be the case when it came to allocating the shift work for the day.

"I was not the only one who had heard singing in the night. Several of the team flat out refused to go down into the shaft without assurances they would be safe from the Wee Folk, assurances, of course, I was both unable and unwilling to provide.

"In the end I got enough of them to go down into the dark to at least get the work started. I gave them the speech, about why we were here in the first place, reminded them of the silver we had already found and our hope for more of the same to be waiting in the rock. I appealed to our bond of brotherhood, we men of the dark and some did respond to my pleas but others only went to work so as not to appear churlish to their friends.

"But surly workers are careless workers. I do not quite know how it came about, I was not at the face at the time but our youngest man, Jake McGinn broke his arm, bad enough that a shard of bone split the skin. When they brought him up out of the shaft, I thought at first he was dead already, for he had fallen into a faint and was as white as a fancy Dublin undertaker's shroud. Then, when he did wake, we could not stop his piteous screaming and even the uisque had little effect, for the wound was sore.

"Of course, my first thought was of the possibility of infection. But without Kelly around to help, we could only clean the wound, patch and stitch the lad up as well as we were able, put a splint on the arm and hope he still has the use of it when he heals, if he lives long enough. At least he passed into a fitful sleep after the bloody work was done, which was a small blessing in a day woefully short of them.

"It did not help that our attention to the lad's arm was watched all along by three more of the damned mannequins, sitting up in a rafter near where the wall met the roof like an attentive audience at a stage play, following our every move intently. I have given up trying to dispose of them, for there are too many now in all corners of the camp and in the surrounding trees and bushes. They proliferate faster than they can be destroyed and the men are starting to see them as talismans of luck rather than any foreboding of doom. They are more likely to blame me for our misfortunes and for that I have Malone to thank once more. There is a reckoning coming between us, one I must prevail in, if I am ever to have the men's trust.

"And there is still no silver in the rock, which remains obdurate and dark, mocking us with its obstinacy against all our efforts.

"It rained incessantly all morning after McGinn's accident, with a strong wind driving it straight down the shaft mouth. It was not too long before water pooled up around the feet of the men at the face. By lunchtime I called off for the day, fearing that to keep the work going would only lead to another accident, or worse, drowning.

"But all I achieved was to have a squad of discontented men huddled together around the stove, drinking uisque and ale and becoming angrier as the liquor took its hold. Any time I caught the eye of a man their gaze slid aside, as if they were afraid to look me in the eye. In their minds I have become the Jonah and I feared they were almost ready to cast me into the belly of the beast.

Seeing the mood of the men to be so taken against me and fearing as I did for all of our lives under the threat of invisible contagion, I too partook of the uisque. I did not drink enough to addle my senses but had more than enough to put a certain distance between myself and our trouble.

"Matters came to a head in late afternoon and once again Malone was the instigator. It began when I found another of those bloody mannequins when I was looking for my pipe. This one was in the pocket of my jacket, although I had not felt anyone placing it there. Putting a hand on it unawares brought all my anger to the surface at once and, emboldened by the uisque, I threw the blasted thing into the stove and demanded to know who was to blame.

"Malone stood nose to nose with me. He turned the blame back on me, echoing his earlier statements that all the misfortunes befalling the camp were to be laid on my head for disrespecting the Wee Folk. I told him to shove his Wee Folk up his arse, then kept my previous promise; I laid him out on his back on the floor of the cabin with two good strong punches to his head.

"I would have given him a kick to keep him down but to my astonishment the crew wrestled me aside. They then took turns to lay into me most sorely, so much so I was barely conscious when they threw me into the storage shed here and locked me inside.

"I am allowed only my writing implements and this journal. I was brought food at supper but no man has spoken to me since the fracas in the cabin and still none will look me in the eye. Before starting this entry, I looked out of the half inch of a gap between the door and the jamb to see Malone strutting and preening like a peacock on the porch of the main cabin, with the men hanging on his every word. The only satisfaction I could take was that he sported a bruise the size of an egg on his left cheek; it will surely blacken nicely on the morrow.

"I could not make out much of what he was saying but fear it is more of his tales of faerie and goblin, auld gods and auld country. He has them all believing it and they are lost to any plea I might make for rationality. Besides, I am not sure rationality is of any use to me now, for enforced confinement is not the sum total of my misfortunes this day.

"I have left the worst of it to the last. My punches, while they felt good and just and proper as I was delivering them, have left me with scraped and torn knuckles on my right hand. It was only when I took to writing this entry and noted the stiffness there I thought to examine the wounds.

"I left it too late to wash and clean the cuts, far too late, although in truth I doubt if it would have made any difference to the fate now awaiting me. There is a black tracery, a spider web all over the back of my hand and I feel it creeping toward my wrist even now as the fingers stiffen.

"If I had a knife I might attempt to cut it out but I can see by the light of my candle that it has already spread too far. And besides, I saw what was inside Malone's wound when Kelly cut him. I fear I do not have the strength to look into my own body and see nothing but dry wood where a man should be.

"Now as I write this, what might be my last entry, there is a mannequin sitting by my right hand that was not there when I began to write, although no one has entered the room in the interim. Its emerald eyes mock me and I have not the energy to do anything but watch it and listen to it as it sings.

My bonnie lies over the ocean, my bonnie lies over the sea,
My bonnie lies over the ocean, oh bring back my bonnie
to me.

"I am afraid I will never be returning across the ocean to my auld home. I am afraid I can only sit here as this black thing grows in me. I am afraid to die. My last entreaty is one for mercy.

"God help me. God help us all."

Keith looked up from the journal, distracted by a sudden noise. The Professor slept on, head back, breathing softly, thankfully not snoring but that wasn't it. Then it came again, the rustling, like dry leaves in the wind, a sound he couldn't pinpoint but was the same sound he'd heard in his apartment the night before. The waiting room had blinds on the windows, currently closed but Keith thought if he opened them, he'd look out to see a pair of green eyes staring back in.

And if I did that, I might well go completely mad.

He sat still, holding his breath, for long seconds but the noise wasn't repeated. When he finally remembered to breathe it was almost a sob and it was several more minutes later before he finally went back to the journal.

He wasn't surprised to note he'd arrived at the last few pages with anything written on them. The handwriting sprawled across the paper in far from straight lines. It was almost illegible in places but he got the gist of it well enough.

"July 11th

"I have not been fed today but it scarcely matters for I am now sure this is my last day on this earth. My veins are black all through my forearms and I suspect higher than that, although I do not have the bravery to investigate beneath my shirt. My hand is stiff such it pains me to write but I must put down here all that has happened this day, for it is a tale needing to be told. When it is done I shall put this journal in the box with the rest of the papers. What happens to it then I leave to history to resolve for by then I shall be long past caring.

"After I wrote my entry last night I went to sleep on top of the bags of flour in the corner, fully expecting not to wake up. I had finally made my peace with the Almighty on my knees for most of the previous hour, as pious as any priest of Rome and I slept the sleep of the just in a green place where my dreams were all of the pleasant variety. For a time, I was even content.

"To my great surprise I woke to see sunshine in the gap under the door. There was no sound; not a bird sang, I felt no discernible wind and, worst of all, the whole camp had fallen deathly quiet and still. Even poor McGinn's pained moaning had fallen silent.

"At first, I thought I had awoken either too early for breakfast, or too late but in that case, I would have excepted to be fed and watered at least. But when I called out through the gap in the door no one replied. The porch of the main cabin was empty. The door was closed and it looked like it was going to remain that way no matter how much I shouted.

"I hammered, long and hard, against the unyielding wood

but the door stood, a combination of its sturdy build and my ever-increasing weakness in the face of the black growth coursing through me. I know not how long I shouted and wailed for attention but by the end of it I was once more on my knees, full weary on the floor by the door with one eye staring through what little gap there was to the rest of the camp beyond. The sun was now high in the sky and yet there was no reply to my entreaties, no movement. It felt like the whole of creation suddenly stood still.

"Then I heard it, the sound of dry leaves being stirred in a breeze. At first, I thought the rustling was somewhere in the shed alongside me, for it sounded like it came from everywhere yet nowhere but when I forced myself to stand and search the room I found nothing but myself and the camp stores.

"A shadow moved beyond the door and I cried out in relief, falling to my knees again in supplication. The rustling sound grew louder still and I saw the shadows were not solid of the kind cast by a man. Rather, these were shifting and dancing, reminding me of nothing else but trees and the patterns cast on a wall by wind and moonlight.

"I pressed my face against the gap in the door and looked out. That single moment was when I knew for certain, today is to be my last.

"Kelly has returned to camp; what is left of him.

"I only knew it was Kelly because his trousers and boots were still in place, although the pants were little more than tattered rags covering what was underneath. The entire upper half of the body was a twig, branch, and leaf representation of the man he had been, a life-size version of the mannequins that have so plagued me these past days.

"'Kelly?' I whispered and the impossible head, made bearded with greenery, turned slowly toward the door as if it could see me through the wood. I could not breathe as I looked into his face; there was nothing of the man I'd known there, nothing of any humanity whatsoever. The eyes were the worst I think, being no more than pinpricks of green emerald dancing with an internal flame. He pointed at me with his right arm, what remained of it, it being strangely elongated, a single long dark twig. The sight of it chilled me to the bone and I backed away from the door. I heard him moving and rustling immediately outside.

"'Kelly?' I said again. 'Help me. For pity's sake, man.'

"But my plea was ignored completely. The rustling of leaves got louder again as the figure moved away. I went back to peer out of the door but he was already out of my sight. I saw the shifting shadow for long seconds, heading up onto the porch of the main cabin. It pushed its way in through the door and was almost immediately lost from my sight, then all was quiet once more.

"I have sat here for the length of this long day now, watching, waiting for the thing Kelly has become to return and take me. But the camp is quiet, as quiet as I soon will be.

"I wish I could go down the shaft one last time to have a hack at the rock and see the silver I know has to be there. But it is not to be. My fingers no longer serve me and I can write no more, let alone wield a pick.

"I shall lock this journal in the iron box and pray my words go ahead into a future I will not know. My time here is done. But I refuse to become the impossible thing I saw in Kelly's form. I have a candle, matches and plenty to burn.

"If you are reading this, light a candle of your own and say a prayer to your God.

It might be the only thing to save your soul.

"I leave you now to go to save mine."

18

Gerry floated, lost in the green. In some remote part of his mind he knew this was the sedative doing its job and giving him distance from the horror. That was his rational mind talking and increasingly he mistrusted that part, relying instead on instinct, which told him this too was real, this endless vista of wafting, drifting foliage with no up or down, left or right, only a warm sea of green.

He didn't know how long he'd been here; he didn't care for he felt safe and didn't have to look at monsters. What else did a lad need? Somewhere in the distance was a rhythmic thudding, the dialysis machine, something else he knew rationally but dismissed immediately; that was back there in the room where bad things happen, the place he wasn't going to think about for a while.

For now, he was more than content to drift and even manage to find some kind of calm.

This is much better.

It wasn't to last though. The foliage he drifted through thinned, showing darker patches beyond as if he had found a direction and was purposefully heading toward something.

Or being drawn.

The foliage yellowed at the edges, an all too solid reminder of the mannequins he wanted to forget. The wood itself, twig and branch, took on a dry dead look even as it parted ahead to show his destination.

No. Please, not here.

Suddenly the hospital room didn't seem so bad after all, at least in comparison to the twin dark holes of the mineshafts in the rock face directly ahead of him. He closed his eyes, or tried to, but even if he had eyes, they weren't obeying orders. He wasn't drifting now; there was definite intent in his movement, an invisible force tugging him forward and down into the dark hole of shaft two.

Any warmth and wellbeing he felt washed away as a cold draft hit him like a slap in the face with a wet towel. A frigid dampness seeped down into the heart of him and black filled where green had been seconds before. He couldn't hear the thud of the dialysis machine. It was silent, a deadened, muffled silence without echoes or murmurs. There was only the cold and the dark and a feeling of falling, downward, into the black.

My Bonnie lies over the ocean.

The song came up from below, faint at first, growing stronger as he descended toward a flickering light, brighter as he approached the lowermost depth of the shaft. Fear surged through him. There was a dark pool of unknown depth ahead; if he sank into it he might never return.

Yeah, bring back, oh bring back, oh bring back my Bonnie to me, to me.

Oh, bring back, oh bring back, oh bring back my Bonnie to me.

It was more than one voice, probably three at least, maybe more. Gerry thought again of bloodied mannequins, sick mothers and he tasted the black liquor in his mouth and throat, smelled vinegar and burnt oil.

As he got closer his eyes adjusted in the dim light and he saw the black pool at the bottom of the shaft. It wasn't doll-like mannequins sitting around it by the light of two small lanterns; it was half a dozen men, all of them bearded with shaggy mops of hair, their clothing strangely old-fashioned. As they sang, the Irish accent came through strong.

Gerry knew immediately what he was seeing. This had to be the original crew, the miners who worked these shafts. His downward movement halted and he hovered, almost six feet above the men's heads as they sang, bringing the old song to its climax. Then they passed round a whiskey bottle, each taking a long slug before one of them spoke. Gerry heard everything said, clear as day, although he knew he would never be able to converse with them in this place; he had been brought here specifically as a witness.

"So, what now, Malone?" a dark-haired man said in his thick Irish accent. He was dressed in thick heavy cotton dungarees caked in dirt. His arms, bare under the garment, showed black veins tracing all the way from fingers up to biceps. Gerry looked around and saw all of them were similarly afflicted, with some of them showing the tracery all the way up to their necks.

Malone, a hefty bearded man with a fresh bruise all over the left side of his face took another slug of whiskey before answering. The black veins crawled across the back of his hands like tiny earthworms under the skin.

"It's all bastard Donnelly's fault that things haven't gone well for us, lads, what with him disrespecting the auld ways like he does. Well, he can sit and rot in the bloody shed for the rest of the summer and if he thinks he's having a share of the spoils, he can think again. Now we're free of his hard-headedness. Now we work. The silver's there in the rock, waiting for us. The Wee Folk wouldn't be here otherwise."

The first man spoke again, lifting up his arms to show the black tracery there.

"No, I mean, what do we do about this? This is some special kind of fuckery right here. Are we all going to die?"

Malone's laugh rang out loud, echoing and booming around the enclosed chamber and setting the candles in the lanterns flickering. He held up his own hands.

"This is a blessing, lads, a sign the Wee Folk are with us. Drink, sing and be happy. We'll have at the silver in the morning and the work will go well, as long as we keep our benefactors happy. Trust me."

He took another slug at the whiskey bottle, then poured a generous amount into the pool where it swirled gold against the black for a second before it was gratefully swallowed.

The bottle got passed around again and they all sang, something about leaving Liverpool, a song Gerry vaguely knew but not well enough to follow it as it was being sung in the thick Irish accents. The chorus echoed around the mineshaft for long seconds after the singing had stopped. Silence fell again as they opened another bottle of whiskey. Despite the tracing of black in their veins, the men seemed quite content, almost happy.

After a time one of the others spoke again addressing Malone.

"Here, Pat, I canna feel my legs."

"You shouldn't have had so much hard liquor, boy. You haven't had the practice."

"No, I mean it, Pat. There's something wrong with my legs."

"Don't talk daft, man. What could be wrong with your legs down here? You're not even using them. All you're doing is sitting on your arse."

The man who had spoken pulled up the leg of his trousers. The flesh underneath looked more like rough bark than skin and when he rapped at it with his knuckles the sound was hollow and dull, as if he'd knocked on a door.

"What is this shite?" the man said.

But by then the rest of them were too busy with their own problems.

Gerry watched it all as if it was happening in fast forward in a time-lapse video. It took them fast.

Their legs went first, twig and bark and branch and leaf bursting through skin, muscle and clothes. There was no blood to speak of, as the foliage sucked it up, the green taking the red and subsuming it. The men's screams were terrible to hear but not one of them moved from their seat around the pool; their legs were literally rooted to the spot, held to the rock by a myriad white, woody tendrils.

Veins, arteries, sinews, bone and tooth, all went, an inch at a time as the men screamed. Then even the screaming stopped as throats filled with leaf and twig and tongues hardened to wood. Malone's beard sprouted buds, then leaves quickly furling open to spill down his chest, a green flood finally taking all there was of the man away, even as the song rose up again in the mineshaft as if from everywhere and nowhere.

Yeah bring back, oh bring back, oh bring back my Bonnie to me, to me.

Oh bring back, oh bring back, oh bring back my Bonnie to me.

Malone's right eye was the final thing human to go, eaten through in seconds by a writhing mass of twig and root and leaf. As the last note of the song faded the only sound was the faintest of rustling, as leaves shifted in the slightest of breezes.

Gerry drifted upward and away. As he did so he passed another figure standing in the darkness higher up the shaft, a man-sized mannequin. This one wore tattered trousers and pointed down at where the other men sat; pointing with a right hand that was one long dark stick, a stick Gerry recognized immediately.

The force propelling Gerry pulled him higher still, up and away from the view.

The green mannequins rose from their seats and lurched up out of the dark behind him, following him back up and out of the shaft.

All that was left around the pool was the flickering lanterns and the whiskey bottles, one of them not quite empty.

11

The Professor woke up not long after Keith finished reading the journal and Keith was glad of the company, for the rustling sound, even faint as it was, had come back and it was driving him to distraction trying to pinpoint the source.

"Not as bad as sleeping in the truck, not as good as a bed," the Professor said, standing to stretch and groaning with the effort. "How long was I out?"

"Long enough for me to finish reading the diary entries, not long enough for you to start snoring."

"And now do you agree with me there's only the one possible explanation?"

"I might, if I get a chance to think about it for a bit longer. But for now, I have a question," Keith said, tapping at the laptop screen as he spoke.

"Only the one?"

"One that feels important anyway. And it's assuming Donnelly did what he said he was going to do. If the box of documents was inside the cabin when he self-immolated and burned it down, how did it get where you found it?"

"Things move over time," the Professor replied. "You're an archaeologist. You know that."

"Yep. But if it was moved why wasn't it opened and who moved it and…"

The Professor stopped him.

"We might never know. You know that too, or you should. And here's a better question and one I've been considering for a while. What if it was moved deliberately knowing we'd be the ones to find it?"

Keith had to think about his response.

"Are you suggesting there's somebody behind all of this? Everything that's happened and is happening, is not random and there's a motivating force? Something with enough intelligence to lure us into a trap?"

"You've read the journal now. What do you think?"

"To be honest, Professor, I'm not sure I can believe it. This supernatural stuff is a bit far out there for you, isn't it?"

"For both of us, I'm sure. But what other conclusions can we draw?"

"So, you think what? The miners called up something out of the mine and it turned them into flesh-eating branches and twigs and big fucking wooden dolls?"

That got Keith another weary smile.

"It's either that or we're both going mad in exactly the same fashion," the older man replied. "What are the odds?"

Keith didn't get time to reply. The doctor in charge of their procedures arrived in the doorway and the look on his face was enough to tell Keith their troubles had only started.

II We need to talk," the doctor said.

"It looks more like you need to talk and we need to listen," the Professor replied and the doctor nodded. The man looked tired, worn out. More than that, he looked worried.

"What is it?" Keith asked. "Are we infected?"

"No, you're both clear, as far as we can tell, although I don't know why. The problem lies elsewhere. It's the nurse, your partner Joanna. She's got what the lad in Gander had."

The doctor kept talking but Keith couldn't process it. His heart pounded, blood rushed in his ears and if he hadn't been sitting, he'd most probably have fallen over. It took him a while to articulate so much as a word.

"And the baby?" The Professor gave him a sharp sideways glance but Keith had no time for explanations. "Is the baby okay?"

The doctor was quiet for so long Keith feared the worst.

"We're doing all we can, for both of them."

That's not enough.

He thought it but didn't say it. He knew the stresses medical staff worked under and he also knew it wasn't a job he'd ever want.

"Can I see her?" he asked, trying to keep his voice calm and not quite succeeding.

"Of course. She asked for you earlier but that was before..."

"Before what?" Keith said, almost shouting now but he knew the answer.

Before she went down into unconsciousness. Like Gerry did.

The doctor confirmed his suspicions.

"She's stable but I'm afraid she's non-responsive."

"That's exactly what happened to Gerry but he woke up after dialysis, didn't he? That'll work here too?"

"That's what we're hoping for," the doctor said and again Keith fought back the urge to snap at him.

Hope is all any of us have got.

Five minutes later he stood at the door of a room two floors above, looking in through the glass to where Joanna was stretched out on a bed, staring sightlessly at the ceiling. He wasn't allowed in until he put on gloves and a mask.

"I thought you said we were clean?" he said to the doctor.

"Yes, as far as we can tell, you are. But she isn't and we haven't identified the pathology of this thing, whatever it is. We don't even know if it's spread by touch, or whether it's airborne. It may even be genetic, which is what they're working on in Gander right now. So, keep the mask and gloves on, don't touch her and definitely no kissing or holding hands. Clear?"

Keith couldn't take his gaze from Joanna. She looked smaller than she should, dwarfed by the bed, pillows, drips and machinery surrounding her too-pale face. Her arms lay above the covers. They weren't pale but were both traced, from fingers to elbows, with the thick black veins he was coming to recognize.

"Are we clear?" the doctor said, louder.

Keith nodded.

"I'm clear."

He stepped through into the room when the doctor opened

the door. Every part of him wanted to rush to the bedside and gather her in his arms but he couldn't risk it.

I might make matters worse. This is my fault.

"I'm here," he said, not knowing whether she could hear him but needing to speak anyway. "They say the baby's okay."

She didn't blink and her heart rate monitor didn't shift from its steady blip. Keith fought back tears, worry, guilt and shame, all at once, welling up inside him.

"I'm sorry."

In his head it all jumbled together; the mannequins in the cabin, Gerry's illness, the dash to the hospital, him buying cigarettes, smoking furtively in the courtyard and the green-eyed thing in the birch tree. They'd all been part of a timeline, a series of events leading directly here, to the side of this bed and to him facing up to something he should have faced long ago.

"I'm here," he said. "And I'm yours, if you'll have me."

He took the cigarette packet from his pocket, crunched it in his hand and dropped it in a waste bin at the side of the door.

"That's it. I'm done with that."

As he said it, he knew he meant it. As he stood there, impotent against the infection running through the woman he loved, he also knew something else.

He would return to the campsite as soon as he got out of here. It was time to put a stop to all of this, once and for all.

12

Gerry came out of the dark and into the light, blinking at the sudden brightness of the overhead fixture in the hospital room after what had felt like a prolonged period of darkness.

"Mom?" he said as a figure moved in the chair to his right.

"No, it's me, son," his father answered. "How are you feeling?"

You mean, do I see any little green men running around? Not at the moment, thanks for asking.

Gerry kept quiet. His dad didn't go in for flippancy at the best of times.

And this is a long way from that.

Besides, he saw by the look on the man's face that his dad was bone tired and more, he looked five years older than the day before. There was no trace of the black veins, no sign dad had been infected but worry etched deep grooves at the corners of his eyes and they were red-rimmed and moist as if he'd been crying.

"What is it, dad?" Gerry asked, then, panic rising again inside, "and where's mom?"

It looked like the man was about to burst into tears.

It's bad. It's worse than bad.

"I hadn't decided whether to tell you," dad said and Gerry heard the sob in his voice, a sound he'd never heard before and hoped never to hear again.

"Dead?" Gerry said, barely more than a whisper.

"No. Not yet."

Those last two words were like a dagger to Gerry's heart. He sat up fully in the bed.

"Take me to her."

"You shouldn't be moving."

"Fuck that," Gerry said and realized it was the first time he'd ever sworn in front of his old man. It was a sign of how far gone in worry the man was that it didn't even seem to register. Gerry held up his arm, drawing attention to his feeds and drips. "Get a nurse to get this shit off me or I'll tear it out myself."

His father finally got agitated at that.

"You shouldn't get yourself worked up, son,"

"It's a bit late for that, dad. Please? I need to see mom. And I think she'd want to see me."

He saw the look passing across his father's face at that.

It's even worse than I thought. What have I done to her?

It took too many, too long, minutes to persuade a nurse he hadn't seen before and then his doctor that he was well enough to be unhooked from the machines. When he asked after the nurse who had been tending him earlier he got a shake of the head from the doctor.

"She's got what you had too, like your mother. And if your mom weren't next door I wouldn't be letting you out of this room until we get a handle on whatever is going on here."

"I'm contagious?"

Again, the doctor shook his head.

"Every test we've done says otherwise. And I'm not infected. I've been around you more than anyone, even more than your nurse or your mother. Your dad here's fine too. If you're contagious it's not in any way we understand or can track. We're wondering whether there's some genetic effect at play but if there is we haven't identified it yet."

While he was speaking the doctor had unhooked Gerry from the dialysis machine and the drips. Gerry's arm ached, a deep, cold pain like severe toothache and when he swung his legs out of bed and tried to stand he almost fell back onto the pillows straight away as a wave of dizziness and nausea washed over him.

"Take it slowly," his doctor said. "Your system's been through the grinder and you might not be out of the woods yet."

Gerry leaned on the doctor's arm as they went to the door. Now he had stood up, he saw his clothes and his satchel were on a low trestle at the bottom end of the bed; they'd been there all along but out of his sight. He moved toward them but the doctor wouldn't hear of him getting dressed.

"Nope. You get five minutes with your mom, tops, then you come straight back to bed. That's the deal. If you don't like it you can go back to bed right now."

"I'll take it," Gerry said. Having the gown flapping at his bare ass for the world to see was a price he would gladly pay. He wanted, needed, to see his mom.

It was worse than he feared.

His mother lay on her back, staring unseeing at the ceiling. A dialysis machine thumped and thudded in the corner and she had the same variety of drips and feeds hooked up to her left arm Gerry had had taken from his own. His gaze kept going back to her right arm. It had gone almost black, with a tinge of green evident in the thick corded veins running all across the skin, the mass of twisting woody tissue having spread from the black thorns of her fingernails all the way up to her shoulder.

"Isn't the dialysis working?" Gerry whispered.

"Not as well as it did for you. We're only slowing the progress of the infection, not stopping it. If it reaches her brain…"

The doctor didn't finish the sentence; he didn't have to.

Gerry stepped forward toward the bed. The doctor held him back.

"No closer, son. She can't see or hear you anyway."

"I could… I mean, when you all thought I was non-responsive. I saw and heard everything."

The doctor looked skeptical but Gerry didn't care what the man thought. Mom would hear him, he was sure of it.

"I'm here, mom. And I'm better. That means you'll get better too, so hang in there and let them work on you. I know you can hear me. Don't you dare die."

A high-pitched laugh came from somewhere in the room. If the doctor heard it, he didn't respond, even when the voice, which was heavily accented and Irish, spoke.

"She's in the green with the auld family now, lad. If you don't like it, you shouldn't have taken the stick."

Gerry knew better than to reply to a voice only he could hear. All it would get him was tied to a bed and drugged into insensibility. He didn't have time.

He leaned forward toward his mom again.

"You hear me, mom? Don't you dare die."

The doctor tried to pull Gerry away, back toward the door. Gerry brushed him off.

"You shouldn't touch me. You don't know where I've been."

He listened again, expecting the Irish voice to have something to say but there was nothing else; he'd been told what had needed to be told.

I shouldn't have taken the stick. This is my fault.

He had one last look at his mom.

"I'll fix this, mom. I'll fix you. I promise."

As he turned to leave the Irish voice laughed again, a cold thing with little humor in it but it didn't say any more about the stick. It didn't have to.

As Gerry closed the door he heard the song start up again. It sounded like there were three voices.

Bring back, oh bring back, oh bring back my bonnie to me, to me.

Gerry was shown back to his own room. The doctor left him at the doorway, trusting him to make his own way to bed.

"It looks like you're off the drips and on the mend," he said. "But there's a buzzer by the bed if you need it. I'm not going anywhere until we get the others back to where you are now."

Gerry was left alone in the room. He listened carefully to see if the doctor would try to keep him in but he didn't hear a lock being engaged from the other side. There were blinds on the inside of the door and he closed them; he didn't want anyone seeing in for the next few minutes. He'd made up his mind while looking at his mom.

I need to get out of here.

He dressed quickly, pleased to find all of his clothes were there in a neat folded pile, although they smelled strange, as if they'd been washed in an astringent disinfectant. He had to sit on the edge of the bed to get his pants, then socks and shoes on; bending down too low brought on a dizzy nausea threatening to spin him away into unconsciousness again. He took it slow although he was aware someone could walk in on him at any moment.

After dressing he stood, having to hold on to the bed to keep him stable. His head swam and his legs felt like he'd been running for miles. When he took a hand off the bed he was able to stay upright, although if he'd been in any kind of wind it would likely have toppled him.

He checked his satchel. He had his wallet, flashlight, a notebook and was relieved to see his tablet was there alongside them and had almost a full charge of power still in it.

He had to make some calls but first he had to get out of the room before his escape plan could be uncovered. As the titular 'patient zero' he knew they weren't going to let him leave, whether he was contagious or not.

He put the tablet in his bag and slung it over his right shoulder. His legs still felt shaky, not quite solid beneath him. He could walk but running was definitely going to be out of the question for a while. He went to the door and opened it an inch, far enough so he saw all the way down the corridor. Somebody spoke next door but it wasn't a conversation, it was his father and he was reading aloud, something from the Bible by the sound of the tone and cadences.

Don't bother with that, dad. It never did me any good, did it?

There was something inherently soothing about his dad's voice, a reminder of better days, long past, when he'd read Gerry stories at bedtime, back in the days before his work almost consumed him and Gerry became a disappointment rather than a joy. He stood listening for several seconds before moving.

Somebody could come along at any moment.

His dad's voice was the only sound he could hear. The rest of the corridor was empty and quiet.

Now or never.

He slipped out the door, closing it silently behind him. A quick glance into his mother's room told him his father was still reading. He sat in the bedside chair but had turned it to face mom, so he had his back to the door; Gerry was able to quickly walk past without being noticed.

A muffled conversation was going on some distance down the corridor but it was well past the doors to the stairwell he came to only a few meters farther on. He went through the door as quietly as he was able and down the internal staircase as fast as he could manage, expecting at any second someone would notice him and call out.

No such call came and he was alone on the empty, echoing stairs. A couple of minutes later he arrived at the foot of the stairwell and had to stop, his breath coming heavy and his vision swimming. He leaned against the wall, forehead pressed against it, waiting for the dizzy spell to pass, not moving until he was sure he could do it without throwing up.

The only door here opened out to another corridor. Going left led to the wide reception area. Gerry went right and, trying to look like he knew where he was headed, kept going, past a small coffee shop and then quickly through a side entrance leading him out into a wide almost empty expanse of parking lot.

It looked to be afternoon. The sun was on its way down to the west and although it wouldn't be dark for hours yet, there was already a chill in the air.

Now what?

13

Keith and the Professor stood by the coffee machine in the corridor outside Joanna's room. They talked in hushed whispers, each of them knowing this wasn't a conversation that needed to be overheard.

"I've been thinking about what the doctor said," the Professor said. "About it being possibly genetic. Joanna's from an Irish background, isn't she?"

"Yes, on her dad's side from way back. Why?"

"Think about it. It has taken the three lads and now Joanna. What do they have in common we don't? The lads told us, back in the truck on the way to the camp. They're all from Irish stock. And we're not."

"It must be a coincidence."

"And all the original Irish mining team too? It's a damned big coincidence in my book. Put it all together and it makes sense."

"Maybe so. But it doesn't help us to do anything about it."

The Professor looked thoughtful.

"Maybe it does. I think we have to go back to the camp and dig deeper. We must have overlooked something important; at least, I hope that's the case. If this is anything more than a random outbreak, if there is something with a plan behind it all, then there's got to be a way to stop it."

Keith could hardly think of anything beyond Joanna's pale face in the hospital room and the small new life in her that was under threat before it had hardly begun. He could see the logic in the Professor's words, though.

And I have to do something.

It was as if the Professor read his mind.

"There's nothing you can do for her here except trust the doctors to do their job."

And that's exactly what she'd want me to do.

"So, we go back to the camp?" he asked. "The two of us, alone?"

"Yes and as soon as possible. In fact, I think we should go right now, if you're up to the drive."

"Your car won't make it up that track. Can we get the truck?"

"All I have to do is put in a request. I can make the call now if you have your phone."

Keith got out his cell-phone. It rang in his hand before he could call up the number.

"Keith," Gerry's voice said at the other end. "We need to talk."

PART 3: THE GREEN AND THE BLACK

1

Gerry sat at the rear of the dark bar in a corner where he could see the main door but should be far enough in the shadows not to be seen. He had a corridor to the men's room to his left and he'd checked it out already; it also led to an Emergency Exit out to the parking lot beyond, a quick escape route should one be needed.

He hoped he didn't have to make a run for it. He'd been on the move for a couple of hours walking the streets of Gander but a combination of cold and increasing fatigue had finally sent him inside in search of warmth and food.

"We'll be with you in four or five hours," Keith had said when he called. So, he still had at least two hours of time to fill and to evade anyone who might be looking for him before Keith and the Professor turned up to head for the campsite. The call had only been a short one but got a sense from Keith's tone there was some urgency and Gerry was glad he wasn't going to have to make his own way back to the dark mine.

Then there was the fact neither Doug nor Bill answered his calls. He'd tried three times each now with no reply, the calls were going straight through to voicemail in both cases. Keith hadn't mentioned them during their short talk.

Maybe they're coming in the truck.

He couldn't believe that. When he thought of the two other students he got a picture of them sick, staring sightlessly at a ceiling as dialysis machines thudded beside their beds. He hoped that was the most they had wrong with them.

There's nothing I can do about it from here.

He ordered a pizza and a beer and settled in for a wait.

Over the next ten minutes his body relaxed. He felt better now he wasn't moving around and even the pain in his left arm where the needles had been was abating. His mind was another matter. His thoughts raced, full of images he couldn't dispel, with his pale, ill mother to the forefront of most of them. Then there were the mannequins to consider. At the hospital he was the only one that had seen them and he hadn't had another sighting since his most recent waking.

But it doesn't make them any the less real.

He also kept returning to the last thing said to him in his mother's room at the hospital, the mannequin's words he heard in his head in the same singsong Irish accent.

She's in the green with the family now, lad. If you don't like it, you shouldn't have taken the stick.

Dreams and reality were too close together for him to make any sense of either. He had a growing suspicion he'd made a mistake somewhere along the line and probably more than one. He had no idea how he was going to go about rectifying it. He only knew he had to try, for the sake of his mother's life.

And my own sanity.

He had finished his pizza and was considering another beer when his doctor walked in through the main door of the bar, with two policemen right at his back. Gerry dumped a ten and a twenty beside his plate and sidled off toward the men's room while their backs were turned at the bar. Seconds later he was out the emergency door, into the open air and heading fast along the front of the row of shops and business premises bordering the edge of the parking lot.

He didn't look back, didn't dare to, until he reached the far corner of the lot and turned into the dark shadows beyond the last of the shops. There was nobody behind him; he hadn't been spotted leaving, although it was only a matter of time before someone at the bar remembered him from the description the doctor would give.

He still had a couple of hours before he was picked up outside Walmart. He had no idea how many people were out and about looking for him and he was a fugitive in a strange town with only a basic understanding of the street layout.

Nothing to worry about then.

He took a chance and walked quickly across the parking lot toward the larger shopping mall on the other side. He didn't stop in front of Walmart, he was far too early and it would be too dangerous to hang around there for hours when people were actively looking for him. He kept walking past the store, trying to keep to shadows wherever possible and came to a darker copse of parkland past the looming building, a small circle of trees encircling a kids' playground, quiet and empty at this time of night.

He sat on a bench under the shadows of the birches and huddled close inside his jacket, trying both to keep warm and to look as small and inconspicuous as possible in the dark.

He sat for almost twenty minutes until he felt safe. He took a risk and got out his tablet, dimming the display and holding it close to his chest so that the minimum amount of light would leak out to give him away.

He tried phoning Doug and Bill again but there was still no answer. He didn't try Keith; he hoped they were well on their way up the length of the island toward him by now and didn't want to do anything to slow down their approach. He thought about phoning his father, letting him know everything was okay.

But what would I say to him that would help? He'd think I was deluded.

Gerry's life had taken a sideways lurch, from steady middle class A grade student with a normal, or as close to it as he could hope for, family to Typhoid Mary on the run from the authorities in a single bound. It might be comical if it wasn't quite so surreal and if it wasn't for the fact his mom was lying in the hospital in a coma.

I've got to fix this.

The only thing he could think of doing was to get back to the original campsite and try to undo whatever it was that had been done. He was hoping Keith and the Professor were going to be able to help with that, for Gerry didn't have a clue where to start.

Once again, his thoughts returned to the mannequin's words.

"She's in the green with the family now, lad. If you don't like it, you shouldn't have taken the stick."

But it was a dream.

He was coming to the realization there was no such thing as a dream in this new reality. His world was now a place where wooden mannequins crawled up out of people, old songs were sung where no one else could hear them and Gerry spread the insanity around, purely by touch. The only saving grace was he wasn't infecting everyone and the doctor and his dad were okay.

So far.

Night chills seeped through the bench and into his bones. After one last failed attempt at phoning Bill and Doug, he put his tablet away in the bag and stood, intending to walk around the small play area to get his blood pumping.

Something moved in the tree above him, a rustling, sounding too loud to be wind in the leaves. He looked up. A darker shadow sat overhead in the crook of a branch, small, doll-sized. A pair of emerald green eyes stared straight back at Gerry.

"So, how's this all working out for you, boy?" an Irish voice said, high pitched, almost childlike.

"You're not real," Gerry whispered.

"You don't say?" the figure replied and shifted in the branches to give Gerry a better view of it. He was pretty sure it was the one that had crawled up out of his gut. Whether dream or reality, it felt real enough.

"What do you want from me?" Gerry said.

The little figure laughed.

"What do you want from us? You're the one with the stick."

"I don't know what that means."

"You should have thought of that before you took it. You wanted it badly enough then, didn't you?"

"It was a dream."

"Life is but a dream," the mannequin said. There was more rustling overhead and two more pairs of emerald eyes opened and stared straight at Gerry.

"What do you want from us?" the three figures said in unison.

"I want you to fuck off," Gerry replied, bringing a laugh from the first one that had spoken.

"Ah, lad, there's definitely some Irish in you, isn't there? But if you didn't want the stick, you shouldn't have taken charge of it. Calling up the likes of us comes with a price."

"I've paid. My mother is paying. And the nurse too. How many more?"

"Don't forget your two pals and the lass in the hospital. How many have you got?"

"I don't know what you mean," Gerry said but he had a sinking feeling in his gut.

Things are even worse than I thought.

"What did you mean, calling up. I did no such thing."

That got him another laugh and he tasted the black liquor in his mouth again, felt the same heady surge of it wash through him.

"We chose the place, you decided to take advantage of our hospitality. Then you chose the stick. Now we're here. That's the deal. That's always been the deal."

"Not as far as I was aware."

"Ignorance of the law is no excuse, lad. You're old enough to know that, surely?"

Gerry didn't get a chance to reply. A car alarm went off in the lot past the trees, the wail cutting through the otherwise quiet night air. It only lasted five seconds but when Gerry looked up into the trees overhead again there was only dark shadow and a slight breeze in the foliage.

2

Keith pulled into the bay outside Walmart soon after ten p.m. Fortunately the drive had been an easy one, with only light traffic and clear skies, so they had made good time. The Professor even managed to go back to sleep again and while Keith wanted a cigarette on some of the long empty stretches, he only had to call to mind Joanna's pale face on the hospital bed for all compulsion for a smoke to fade away.

He listened to the radio, tuned in to news rather than music, for fear of waking the Professor There was nothing about the two lads, or what they'd become, in the attic flat of the townhouse. There was, however, plenty of news about Gerry.

People were looking for him. The report said he had left hospital while still under observation, might be contagious, might be seriously ill and might not be in his right mind. The lad who scurried from a copse of trees and ran across the parking lot toward them as soon as they stopped looked to be healthy enough.

"Let's go," Gerry said as soon as he climbed in the back.

"Where to?"

"You knew where. You didn't come all this way only to find me. To the site, of course."

The Professor was still slowly coming awake.

"Are you well enough to travel?" he asked.

Gerry laughed.

"I'm too sick not to. I'm starting to get an idea what's going on here. But first, drive. I've got cops and doctors and God knows who else looking for me and we're running out of time."

The lad obviously knew something, or thought he did but

he was also right. Keith felt it, a sense of urgency, of matters coming to a head. The sooner they got back to the campsite the better.

"Do you need to get something to eat right now?" the Professor asked.

Gerry shook his head.

"Get going. Please? I've been out in the open too long as it is."

Keith drove away, out to the highway, heading west toward the Buchans turnoff then for the track to lead them to the site.

He stopped only when they'd gone through Buchans and had turned onto the track.

"We need a plan," he said. "We can't drive in blind like we did the last time."

"I agree," the Professor replied, turning to Gerry. "It's time we swapped notes and got everything out in the open. Let's start with how you managed to get drunk, Gerry."

It took an hour and more, with stops for questions, answers and recriminations but in the end, they had a narrative worked out, although it wasn't clear to Keith.

"You think this is all because of you, because you took a drink?" he asked Gerry.

"That's what they told me."

"That's what the little green Irish men made out of wood and twigs and leaves told you?" the Professor said and the older man didn't quite keep the disbelief out of his voice. Keith had seen the emerald eyes in the tree. He wasn't so quick to dismiss Gerry's story.

Gerry went quiet when they told him about Bill and Doug.

"I'd guessed as much," he said in barely a whisper. "We've got to get to the camp and do something. My mom's next."

"And my fiancée," Keith replied. "I know we need to hurry. But I'm not keen on setting up camp in the dark."

"We don't have to set up. All we have to do is park and do our thing," Gerry replied.

"Which is what, exactly?"

Gerry took a bottle of whiskey from his satchel and showed

them the label, Bushmills, twelve years old.

"I bought this after my conversation tonight with your little green Irishmen. I think we need to go down into shaft two and have a drink with them."

"Then what?"

Gerry shrugged.

"Who knows. I'm making this up as I go along."

The drive along the track proved to be as torturous as it had been the first time. Whipping branches fought them all the way, deep ruts threatened to bounce them out of their seats if they took it too fast, and an ever-narrowing canopy closed in all around them.

Keith drove in silence; the Professor was lost in thought and Gerry, what little Keith could see of him in the rear-view mirror, looked almost catatonic, wide eyed and staring.

Are we doing the right thing?

Keith was well aware he was heading, with a sick man, back to the place where the sickness had begun and with no real clue as to whether they were about to put themselves into further danger of exposure to contagion. The smart move might be to turn around and deliver Gerry back to hospital.

But it won't help Joanna, not if they don't know what's wrong with Gerry and can't find out in time.

The thought of Joanna and the baby she carried held hostage to fortune kept pushing its way to the front of his mind. If there was even the slightest chance a return to the mine would stop the spread of the contagion and return things to normal, he had to take it. The alternative was to return to her hospital bed, sit there, and wait to see if she died. It wasn't an option he was willing to consider.

The track continued to narrow. If anything, it seemed worse than on the first trip. It hadn't rained but Keith saw signs they'd torn up the ground badly in places on the wild flight back from camp to hospital and the truck's suspension creaked and complained bitterly on some of the bumpier sections.

Finally, as he was thinking the foliage was going to completely close in around them and trap them like an insect in a flytrap, the view opened out and his headlights picked out the flatter, boggy expanse of land beyond.

A few minutes later he drove up onto the drier patch of gravel of their earlier campsite and parked.

3

Gerry was running on instinct. It had been the same back in the playground; after the conversation with the manne-quin, he'd taken a chance and headed for the large Sobeys on the corner of the lot, where he'd waited until the tills were clear, then hurried in to buy the bottle of whiskey. He didn't know why he needed it but all he could think of was the dream of the miners at the bottom of the shaft and the taste of the thick black liquor left in the bottle.

All the way here to the campsite he'd tasted whiskey in his mouth and heard the old songs in his head, the ones the miners sang around the pool. The taste had gotten stronger and more insistent the closer they got and now they were here he had an almost uncontrollable urge to open the bottle and chug it all down.

He sat, hands firmly clasped on top of the satchel and tried to think of his mom, the nurse and now also Keith's girlfriend, all of them infected and all needing him.

Why me?

He knew the answer to that. He was weak, that's why. He'd given in to the call of the bottle the first time without a second thought. Then he'd taken the damned stick. It didn't matter he'd thought it was a dream, it had felt real enough at the time. He'd wanted the swelling emotion of the song, the power that came with the stick. He'd wanted it all. And now he had it and didn't know what to do with it.

The truck's bodywork pinged and creaked as it cooled in the night air. Everything was impenetrable dark except for the patch of gravel and shrubs beyond delineated by the high beams.

"Looks like it's your move, Gerry," Keith said from the front seat and Gerry realized that, far from the two of them knowing what they were doing, the older men were looking to him for guidance.

"Look, this was the best idea I had," he replied. "I haven't a clue as to whether it'll work or not. If you guys have a better one..."

Keith shook his head but the Professor spoke up.

"I don't think it's a great idea to be descending the shaft at night. I know it's illogical, it's dark down there anyway but all the same, I would rather wait for morning. I hoped we might camp out in the old cabin; my back isn't up to sleeping in this seat again. And there might be something we missed in the cabin, something that will help."

I doubt there's anything that will help.

Like the Professor, Gerry didn't relish approaching the shaft in the dark.

But we don't have time to be messing about with archaeology tonight.

He'd hoped the Professor's idea would be more concrete but now he knew the truth; it was down to him to get the job done. He played along though, helping the other two unpack the large LED lanterns from the truck. They took one each and Gerry held back, deliberately slowing to let them get ahead. Once they had entered the denser shrubbery to the south, he took a turn west, heading straight for the rock face and the two dark eye-pits watching him approach.

4

Keith had taken a bearing in the approximate right direction before switching off the truck headlights and heading into the scrub. As before, the ground underfoot was boggy and in the dark it was impossible to see the muddy pools below, so it was a case of plowing through and hoping for the best. He was soaked up past the ankles in cold water within seconds but was actually pleased to see the small, doll-like sculptures looking down at him from the surrounding branches as he got into the denser growth. It meant he was on the right track.

His sense of direction served him well; it only took a matter of minutes to push through the bushes and thin trees and walk into the firmer ground of the clearing. The cabin ahead sat in total darkness and everything was deathly quiet. Keith didn't hesitate; he walked forward, up onto the porch and pushed open the cabin door.

He didn't notice Gerry's absence until after both he and the Professor walked into the room... and after he'd noticed the room was bare. There were no mannequins at the table, or anywhere to be seen. For a split second he had a horrible vision of them all lying, feigning sleep under the covers in the bunks, in the same way as he'd last seen the remains of Bill and Doug. When he lifted the lantern in that direction, all he saw was the bunks and the crumpled sheets.

He turned back to the Professor, noticed Gerry wasn't behind him and knew immediately what the lad must intend.

"Gerry," he shouted and pushed past the Professor, making for the door. He never made it in time. The door slammed shut in his face as if a wind had caught it. It still only hung on the one hinge but somehow it was solidly fixed in the frame and no amount of pushing or pulling from Keith and then both him and the Professor, was going to budge it.

Keith walked over to the nearest window. The shutters, which he remembered had been wide open on their previous visit, were now firmly closed and like the door were as solid and obdurate as if they had been securely nailed shut.

Somebody, or something, doesn't want us to get out.

Both of them put their lanterns down on the table. The lights lit up their faces from below; Keith had once seen a stage magician use the effect in a darkened room to heighten suspense. Here, it accentuated the fright they'd both taken, etching dark shadows into their faces. Keith saw the same fear in the Professor he too felt build inside. Where were the mannequins?

No. They didn't get up and walk. They were moved deliberately. Somebody's playing us for fools.

He couldn't believe it.

He walked round the room trying all the shuttered windows but they were all as firm as the first one. He jumped up and down testing the floorboards, hoping for a weakness, even though he knew there was little to no crawlspace below him. Then he walked round slapping at the walls, checking for a weak spot. Although the wood was old it felt almost as solid as the day it had been built. There was no way out through those hefty logs.

Then he looked up at the rafters, remembering the far end of the cabin's roof had a definite sag in it. He pulled the table over to the end of the room, with help from the Professor when the older man realized what was intended.

When he clambered up onto the table he managed to reach the lowest beam, the main rafter running down the middle of the room but when he tried to put his weight on it the wood creaked and threatened to split. He backed off. He couldn't risk bringing the whole roof down on top of them.

"Pass me up a chair, Professor I should be able to punch through to the shingles from higher up."

"Be careful," the older man said but did as was asked and handed up one of the wooden chairs.

Keith got up on it gingerly. He tested whether it would take his weight and kept one hand on the rafter beam for balance before stepping all the way up onto the chair. Even then it was precarious. He felt off balance and liable to topple at any moment but Gerry was probably down in the mineshaft by now, probably doing something stupid.

Why should he be the only one?

He reached up, still with his left hand on the rafter for balance and pushed at the roof above his head. The wood gave slightly and he heard a tumble and crash as several shingles were loosened enough to fall off. He pushed harder. More shingles fell but the roof held. The wood felt soft and springy to the touch. He punched at it hard and it cracked. The main rafter creaked under his left hand and he held his breath, half expecting to be thrown back down into the cabin as the roof came in.

It held, though, and when he moved his head to one side to let the lamplight illuminate the roof above him he saw an impact mark where his fist dented the wood.

He punched again, harder this time.

5

Gerry stood at the mouth of shaft two with the lantern raised in front of him. The light barely penetrated the blackness. He turned to look back to where they'd parked. With the headlights switched off the truck was just a darker shadow among many and beyond it there was no sign of the others' lights.

Yet again he'd acted on instinct but now he stood here in front of the dark mineshaft mouth, his reason tried to kick in.

What am I planning to do once I get down there?

He still didn't have an answer but the dark emptiness behind him and the lack of sight of the others made his mind up for him. He didn't want to go down the shaft but likewise, he wasn't keen on blundering about in a bog with only a vague idea of the direction in which he should be going. It was either return and sit in the truck, or head down to the black pool.

And only one of those choices gives me a chance of saving my mom.

It was no kind of choice at all.

He held the lantern ahead of him and went down into the dark. Whiskey sloshed in the bottle he had slung in the satchel across his back.

Although he'd been this way before, the fact it was night outside and he was using the LED lantern rather than a flashlight made it feel new and different. The lantern, while not penetrating as far ahead as the flashlight, was bright enough to light more of the rock in his immediate vicinity, making it feel like he descended inside a bubble of light.

He moved slowly, concentrating on where he placed his feet; it wasn't so much he was worried about injury in a fall, it was the fact that if he didn't reach the pool all of it would have been for nothing and more people would die. He couldn't have it on his conscience.

The deeper he got the more he tasted the black liquor in his mouth. There was an accompanying smell now too, one he recognized from last time, vinegar and burnt oil. He passed the graffiti in the rock, Pat Malone, 3rd July, 1874; the Professor had said the man had been mentioned in the diary.

Would all of this have gone differently if I'd read it instead of drinking the liquor?

He might never know.

The smell got stronger and the taste of liquor got almost overpowering. The sloshing of the Bushmills in his satchel reminded him he always had the option of heading back to the truck and drinking until he was blind drunk.

Yeah, because that worked out so well the last time.

He thought of his mom, of the black tracery rampaging through her and kept going down into the darkness.

From somewhere far below the song rose up to meet him and led him onward.

Bring back, oh bring back, oh bring back my bonnie to me, to me.

6

It only took a minute or so for Keith to punch a fist-sized hole in the roof. More shingles clattered away in the darkness outside. He expected to feel fresh air on his face but instead he almost gagged at a thick tang of vinegar and the taste of burnt oil in the back of his throat. He turned his head aside, breathed through his nose and kept punching.

The whole roof shook with his blows, sending dust falling softly down to cover the Professor's gray mop of hair with a fine yellowish-brown crust.

"Careful. You'll bring the whole place down."

"It's stood this long. It can stand for five more minutes."

He kept punching. Large chunks of wood and a few shingles now, fell in on him but not with any great force and he was able to shrug them off easily. Within minutes he had a hole he reckoned was big enough for him to get through.

To do so he was going to have to hoist up onto the big rafter, the same one that had creaked and threatened to split when he'd put his weight on it minutes earlier.

"How strong are you feeling, Professor?" he shouted down.

"It depends on what you want me to do."

"Can you get up on the table and take at least some of my weight while I try to get up out of here?"

"Do I have a choice?"

"Not that I can see. Not if we want to stop Gerry getting into more trouble."

The table, the chair and Keith on top all took a sideways lurch, nearly toppling the whole lot on top of the Professor as he used one of the other chairs to step up onto the table. Keith was able to stabilize both of them by taking a firmer hold on the rafter. It creaked again in his hand, which didn't bode well for his next move.

"On the count of three, I'm going to pull myself up onto the big rafter," Keith said. "At the same time, you need to get up on the chair and try to take some of my weight, as much as you can manage. It should only be for a second until I boost myself up through the hole."

"Sounds simple enough," the Professor said deadpan. "What could possibly go wrong?"

Once the Professor was steady on the table Keith counted out to three and lifted. The rafter creaked and cracked like a gunshot. It bowed alarmingly and sagged down several inches under his foot and the whole roof structure swayed like a yacht in a sudden swell. By then Keith had reached up again and using both hands hauled up and out and onto the roof, dislodging a large patch of shingles in the process. The noise felt suddenly too loud, too intrusive and it was noticed.

As soon as the clatter of the falling shingles died away, he heard it, the sound he'd been hearing these past few days, rustling, like crumpled paper, or dry leaves in the wind.

It was closer.

Keith stretch out flat on his belly on the roof, trying to spread his weight, aware it might give way under him at any moment. He looked down into the hole. The Professor was three feet below, not looking up but looking back across the cabin, in the direction from where the noise was coming.

"I think there's something at the door."

I think so too.

The Professor got off the chair, picked up one of the lanterns then, unsteadily, climbed back up and handed the light to Keith.

"I'll get the other one," the Professor said but he didn't seem convinced and the rustling sound from the door got louder, more frenzied.

Something knows we're trying to escape. And it doesn't like it.

"Leave it. Come on, old man, let's get you out of there."

"On three again?"

"On three. Let's go."

There was a scratching sound now, one quickly turning into a pounding, shaking the whole cabin.

"Three," the Professor said and pulled up onto the rafter left handed while stretching out his right toward Keith, who managed to grab the offered hand in time as the old timber finally gave way under the Professor's weight.

The whole cabin bucked and swayed again and the roof fell in by nearly a foot. Keith felt his grip slipping.

"Your other hand, quick. I can't hold you like this for long."

Down below the cabin shook again, with a bang.

Keith saw the Professor glance to the doorway, then start scrambling, trying to get up higher. Finally, Keith had hold of both hands and was able to pull the Professor up while sliding backward, hoping his legs made enough friction to stop them both being pulled back down.

"Faster," the Professor shouted, with a sudden panic in his voice. "They're here."

Keith took all the Professor's weight, trusted to luck, and heaved. The older man came up out of the hole like a cork out of a bottle but not without a price. The older man yelled, a scream of pain and when they both rolled away from the hole there was blood, dark in the dim light, at the Professor's ankle.

"Did you catch it on something."

"No," the Professor said, looking back at the hole, "I think something caught me."

A huge mass of twig and branch and leaf came up out of the hole and turned. A wide face with an even larger green beard below turned to look at them. From sunken dark eye sockets a pair of emeralds flashed.

7

Gerry wasn't sure what to expect when he reached the bottom of the shaft; he wouldn't have been surprised to see the miners, or at least their mannequins, sitting around the pool sharing a last drink. There was only the cold, dank, dark, smelling of vinegar and burnt oil. The singing had stopped when he was about to enter the final cavern at the deepest point and he imagined he heard it, echoing around him, as he put the lantern down at the side of the pool.

Well I'm here. Now what?

He sat on the edge of the pool, trying to ignore the cold from the rock seeping into his buttocks. His legs dangled over the edge, his feet inches above the sheer, almost glass-like, surface of the pool. There was a ledge of rock some eight inches or so lower he could sit on and actually have his feet in the pool but it wasn't a step he felt like taking.

Not yet.

He unslung his satchel, reached in and took out the Bushmills bottle. The liquor inside looked black and thick in the light from the lantern.

Like the last time.

Also like the last time, he tasted it in his mouth before he even opened the bottle, felt the urge, the need to take a deep swallow.

He turned the screw top, breaking the seal and took a long gulp, sending fiery heat and sudden wellbeing gushing through him. Before he knew what he was doing he had raised his head and sang.

My Bonnie lies over the ocean. My Bonnie lies over the sea.

My Bonnie lies over the ocean. Oh, bring back my Bonnie to me.

His hand, where it gripped the bottle, felt stiff. It didn't surprise him in the slightest to see the black tracery running like tiny snakes all across his knuckles.

Bring back, oh bring back, oh bring back my Bonnie to me, to me.

8

The bearded mannequin climbed up out of the hole in the roof. The whole building swayed and rocked again, as if taken by a wind and Keith heard timbers creak and crack under their feet. The mannequin never took its emerald stare off Keith and Professor It came fully up out of the cabin and rolled into a crouch, foliage rustling, branches creaking, before standing upright, only six feet from Keith. In the dim light it looked like a broad, heavily muscled man silhouetted against the dark sky, the only light being the flash of the emerald eyes.

"Run," the Professor shouted.

As a plan, it had the benefit of simplicity.

"This way," Keith replied and headed for the top of the porch above the cabin's doorway. Even in the three steps it took to get there he was aware the Professor wasn't moving easily, limping and listing badly to one side. He switched the lantern to his left hand, got his right shoulder under the older man's arms and jumped at the same time as the bearded mannequin clumped across the roof behind them, long, twiggy fingers reaching, trying to grab at hair or clothes.

To Keith's surprise, the porch roof held their weight but it was on a slope. They slid forward too quickly to get traction and fell the seven feet to the ground, hitting the gravel with a crunching thud, the impact reverberating through Keith's body like a hammer blow.

At least Keith managed to stay upright; the Professor's landing didn't go so well. His injured leg gave way below him and Keith couldn't handle the sudden, off-balance lurch to one side. The older man fell on his knees on the gravel as the bearded mannequin came down from the porch, climbing down the support timbers like a fast-growing piece of trailing ivy before standing upright in front of them.

Keith swung the lantern straight-armed, aiming at the thing's head. It caved in the whole right-hand side but within seconds the foliage had twisted and ran, filling in the hole with twig and leaf almost as quickly as it had been made.

Keith didn't know how he knew but he knew the bearded thing was smiling now as it came forward again. At least his action had given the Professor time to get to his feet. He tugged at the older man's arm and they staggered away across the clearing.

The mannequin followed.

They fled through the boggy shrub with Keith taking the lead, hoping he'd chosen the right direction. They were making so much noise splashing through the muddy pools he couldn't hear any pursuit but he didn't look back.

If the blasted thing is following us we'll know about it soon enough.

He was relieved after a few minutes of trudging through the sucking bog to see the outline of the truck up the incline ahead of them.

"Get in the truck," he said to the Professor "I'll find Gerry."

When he looked back from the man to the truck he saw their way was already blocked. Three more of the woody mannequins stood between them and the vehicle, three pairs of emerald eyes, gazes fixed on the two men.

The only sound in the night was the dry rustling of leaves as they came forward.

9

Gerry took another drink and this time he also poured some down into the pool.

"Thank you, lad," an Irish voice said and Gerry looked up to see three small mannequins sitting across the pool from him.

"Let me guess, Curly, Larry and Mo?"

His words were slurred and his head felt detached from the rest of him. The black tracery ran all over his hands and up both wrists into his forearms, stiffening the fingers now, so much so he had to use both hands to lift the bottle to his lips.

"Well. I'm here," he said. "What now?"

"That's up to you," the mannequin replied. "You took the stick. You get to decide what to do with it. That's the law. You're a law-abiding lad, aren't you?"

"What about my mother?"

"What about her? If you do the right thing, she'll be fine. If you do the wrong thing, she won't. Same as it ever was."

"And what's the right thing?"

"That's the question I can't answer. You need to figure it out yourself. It's..."

"... the law. Yeah, I get it."

Gerry shared another drink with the pool.

18

It only took a few seconds for Keith and the Professor to realize they were being herded like a pair of recalcitrant sheep. The three mannequins by the truck stopped coming forward at the same time as the hefty, green bearded one who Keith guessed had, at one time, been Malone, came out of the scrub heading for them. When Keith and the Professor moved back all four of the mannequins moved forward. Two more came up onto the flat campsite from the pond side, blocking all flight in that direction.

"What now?" Keith asked, keeping his voice low. "Do we make a run for it?"

"I don't think I'm going to be running anywhere," the Professor replied. He reached for the lantern and guided Keith's arm to cast the light on his wounded leg. Even through the tattered remnants of his pants Keith saw the black tracery, already running rampant up the older man's ankle.

"But you're not Irish," Keith said and the Professor laughed.

"I don't think it gives a fuck, in this place, where it's strong."

"So, what do we do?"

"I get a feeling we don't get much choice in the matter."

The mannequins kept herding them, in tighter formation now as they approached the rock face. Within a few minutes they had Keith and the Professor backed up with the mouth of shaft two looming behind them.

More of the mannequins came up out of shaft one and Keith remembered the Professor's story about the sculpture blocking the passageway. It wasn't a sculpture now; they were mobile, ten at least of them pressing up close and blocking all avenues of escape.

The only way was down.

11

Gerry was lost in the drink somewhere short of comatose but still capable of rational thought, although it was a struggle to fight the call of the soft green dreamscape waiting for him.

Strangely, the mannequins were becoming drunk at the same rate and were joining their voices in song with his.

Bring back, bring back, oh, bring back my bonnie to me, to me.

"Gerry?"

The sound of a familiar voice brought him back to reality with a start. The cavern got brighter as Keith and a limping Professor arrived in the mouth of the shaft. They sidled in, moving away from the entrance and Gerry saw why seconds later as the mannequins arrived right behind them, filling the whole mouth of the shaft with foliage, twig and branch.

"Meet the gang, for the gang's all here," the small mannequins sang.

"Shush," Gerry said.

"I didn't say anything," Keith replied and Gerry, even in his near stupor, remembered he was the only one who saw and heard the small ones.

The bigger mannequins were a different matter. They crowded into the shaft entrance, starting to fill the cavern with rustling foliage and branches.

"What the hell are you doing?" Keith asked. "Give me the bottle."

Gerry saw the Professor hold the other man back and put a finger to his lips. Everything went quiet again except for the soft rustling of leaves and creaking of branches.

"The old man is wise," the small mannequin said. "It's make your mind up time, lad. What's it to be?"

Gerry slid on his backside, over the lip of the pit, to sit with his legs dangling in the black pool. Icy cold immediately gripped his ankles but he had a cure for that. He took another long gulp from the whiskey bottle then poured most of what was left into the pool before carefully placing the bottle down next to his lantern. The Bushmills had an inch of black liquor left in it.

"Same as it ever was," he said and the three small mannequins recited it back to him, as if it was a prayer.

"My mother will be okay?" he asked. "And the others too?"

"All manner of things will be well," the mannequin said and Gerry smiled.

The soft green dreamscape was calling strongly to him now but he had one thing still to do and for the last time his instinct knew what was needed before he processed the thought.

He raised his left hand. His index finger had grown almost a foot long and become all wood, dark and gnarled with the bark beginning to peel off. He pointed it at the nearest of the tall mannequins, then at the pool, repeating the gesture to make sure his point had been made.

The foliage figure stepped forward, the green leaves already going yellow then quickly dry and brown as it stepped into the black pool and was swallowed up, leaving only an oily residue of dust on the surface.

One by one they came; Gerry waved the stick and the mannequins went into the pool with a rustle of dead leaves and scarcely a ripple on the dark surface of the water, until only the burly, green bearded one was left. It held out a hand. Gerry knew what was being asked. He could pass the stick over to it and walk away from here. He remembered the small Irish mannequin's words.

If you do the right thing, she'll be fine. If you do the wrong thing, she won't. Same as it ever was.

He pointed the stick at the green bearded man and then into the pool. The mannequin looked ready to disobey but its foliage was already yellowing. The great beard went almost red, then brown and parts of it fell to the cavern floor as the figure finally moved, stepping forward and lowering itself into the water without a splash. The emerald green eyes flashed twice, staring straight at Gerry then they too were gone.

"Is that it?" Keith said.

"Not yet," Gerry replied. "Tell mom this is for her."

He stretched out his legs, let his buttocks slide off the rock ledge and felt the cold dark take him as he slid away into the soft green faraway places. The last things he saw before his head went under were the three small mannequins sliding into the pool along with him.

All four of them sang as they went down.

Bring back, oh bring back, oh bring back my bonnie to me.

12

Keith pulled away from the Professor's grasp and fell belly first down on the rock, reaching down into the water. The surface was already flat and calm, not a ripple to show where Gerry had gone. He lay there for more than a minute but there wasn't even a bubble of air to mark where the lad might be.

He felt a hand on his shoulder.

"He's gone, lad," the Professor said. "Leave it be."

Keith shuffled backward away from the dark water and stood.

"What happened?"

The Professor looked thoughtful.

"The end of an old story, I think," he said. Keith saw him looking at the Bushmills bottle beside the pool. It still had an inch of dark liquor in it and Keith wondered what it would taste like.

"And the beginning of another if we're not careful," the Professor said. He wasn't looking at the bottle anymore but had rolled his pants up to show Keith his ankle. There were several ugly red puncture wounds but no sign of any black tracery.

"What about the bottle?" Keith asked as the Professor took his arm to lead him away.

"Leave it. This time we're not collectors of history."

"What are we then?"

"We're witnesses."

EPILOGUE

It was morning again by the time they arrived back in St. Johns. A phone call to Gander had eventually garnered them the information that Gerry's mom and his nurse were out of danger and improving but Keith wasn't going to believe it until he saw the evidence. Although he was dog-tired, he drove them straight to the hospital and the Professor was still there, limping by his side as he went up to Joanna's room.

She was awake, sitting up in bed having an ultrasound scan done of her exposed belly but she broke into a broad grin when she saw him.

"Everything's okay," she said. "They say I'm better and the baby's fine."

There was no sign of any black tracery on her arms and Keith felt all the tension and emotion of the past few days well up inside, bringing tears unbidden to the corners of both his eyes.

"The baby's heartbeat's strong," the nurse working the ultrasound machine said. "Do you want to hear it?"

Joanna passed him the headphones to let him hear first. The tears, which seconds before had been as much of relief as of joy, stopped as quickly as they had come and Keith felt the cold of the damp black pool seep into him.

It wasn't a heartbeat he heard. It was a sound he knew would haunt him for the months of the pregnancy to come; rustling, like dry leaves in a breeze.

ABOUT THE AUTHOR

William Meikle is a Scottish writer, now living in Canada, with over twenty novels published in the genre press and more than 300 short story credits in thirteen countries. He has books available from a variety of publishers and his work has appeared in a large number of professional anthologies and magazines. He lives in Newfoundland with whales, bald eagles and icebergs for company. When he's not writing he drinks beer, plays guitar, and dreams of fortune and glory.

Curious about other Crossroad Press books?
Stop by our site:
http://store.crossroadpress.com
We offer quality writing
in digital, audio, and print formats.

Enter the code FIRSTBOOK
to get 20% off your first order from our store!
Stop by today!